The Tohunga of Tarawera

David R Taylor

ISBN 978-0-473-37315-3
National Library of New Zealand

New Zealand, Maori myths & legends, Mount Tarawera

***

The novel is dedicated to my wife Janine, with much love, whose suggestion led to the writing of this book. For this and for her continuous support in the writing of all my novels, thank you.

'There is an undefinable mysterious power that pervades everything.
I feel it even though I do not see it.'

Mahatma Ghandi.

Tarawera

The hand of god has struck the tiger lines
across the face that looks into the sacred pool.
He sees in that dark place the tribal mountain where
his curses have disturbed the air.
The mountain speaks
in orange ash and boiling stone
that will obliterate the place
where water and the crystal meet.
Then will the dry bones of those young men
petrify in ash and turn to dust,
and all his tribe who spat upon his words, must
tremble
as his sacrament will flail the sky in orange rain.

D R. Taylor.

ONE

Whero Taroi sensed a chill, either in the room or in himself. Logic deemed it impossible to see through that which was palpable, yet fragments of what lay outside appeared in brief snatches, seemingly through the walls. The objects, the carvings, the entire substance of the room appeared to dissolve, liquefied into the ether. Solid matter and insubstantial air had begun to merge and it was difficult to tell which was which. The entire room and everything in it was fading, stuff merged with non-stuff, and in the next few seconds Whero found himself on bare ground with the great monolith of Tarawera presented to his vision.

A wave of fire was cascading from the mouth of Tarawera, heading towards the village of Te Wairoa. The corrosive tang of burnt earth stung his nostrils and his short powerful frame braced against the gusts of hot wind generated by the mountain. A blinding flash of light hurt his eyes and a pillar of fire exploded skywards, piercing the clouds that had gathered several hundred feet above Tarawera. The ground juddered and pulsated and its reluctant observer fell to the ground. He looked up as the entire face of Tarawera mountain split open, and another white hot column detonated from the ridge, then another and another. Four white hot cones that had accumulated deep inside the mantle hurled upwards in destructive force as though to seek out and destroy the stars from their ethereal threshold.

Now he saw the great terraces, Otukapuarangi and Te Tarata. Their pools of water began to fill with boiling lava. Deep trenches opened up beneath what had been a thing of indescribable beauty for a thousand years, the shining walls of pink and white sinter cracking open and disappearing into a seething mass of boiling liquid and mud.

The carver tried to close his eyes, vision blurred from the intense heat and smoke, seeing the chaos of his village, dead people, hearing screams as agonised flesh burned. He wanted this premonition of chaos to end. Blackness swallowed him and he fell below the massive statue of the god Maui, inside the meeting house.

He awoke, sensing a presence nearby. His eyes cleared enough to recognise the Tohunga, Tuhoto Ariki, his tall, thin body outlined against the imposing entrance of the Whare Hinemihi. A moment of doubt and possible guilt troubled him as the priest studied the littered fragments of paua that covered the floor. The Tohunga's body was motionless, like the great carvings that guarded the opening.

Aporo, chief of Ngati Hinemihi, had told him it was all right, that it was fine to remove the ancient paua from the eyes of the gods and replace them with the gold coins from pakeha money. The old man had kicked up a terrible fuss, eyes blazing, warning Aporo of a disaster that would follow his actions.

'It is not the gods you please by committing this hara, it is your own vanity.'

Neither he nor Aporo had been born when Tuhoto Ariki had performed the sacred rites, dedicating the ancient carvings to the tribes of Te-Arawa. Although he liked Aporo, Whero had suspected that the Tohunga was right.

The priest, ignoring the carver, looked at the statues of the gods wearing the new coins for eyes. Then he left.

TWO

At this time of day Te Tarata was at its best. A series of white steps, glinting in the declining sun, folded uniformly downward, pouring their beneficent and seemingly unending waters into the lake. At this time also, Te Tarata was spared its incessant visitors: the bathers who slept in its fonts of eternal youth, the doggerel-writing poets, the haggling guides, and the indigenes who lived in nearby Te Wairoa.

The irony was not lost on the cornflower-blue pools, replenished from waters deep within the mantle that flowed over the glowing steps of pure crystal in their passage towards the lake.

A vent of steam at the head of this fountaining cornucopia blew gently skyward, casting its vapour into the ether followed by a powerful exhalation, as though some giant lurked within the boiling cauldron, a restless harbinger that formed a dark cloud floating across the pools. The steam caught up in the green foliage of a tree that existed to one side of the waters, fractured and twisted in its branches, forming intermittent phantom shapes and faces before dissolving into the quantum field of dire possibilities.

The sun had begun its final passage towards oblivion casting its crimson colours across the shine of gold, gradually transformed to flame-red. The blue of reflected water formed within the generous troughs of pink and white sinter had diminished, as though the terraces had taken on the malefic and destructive characteristic of the unusual surge that had preceded today's sunset.

'Nothing lasts,' said the water that for millions of years had cascaded across the land, and its malevolent theme of destruction was taken up in the rock, the hot earth below, the sky, and in the distance the mountain that rumbled its destructive and inexorable message–nothing lasts.

THREE

The solitude of the pink and white terraces was not followed up inside the whare Hinemihi as Keepa, the Rangatira, entered the meeting house. To his left stood the powerful tribal Tuhongu of Te Wairoa. Keepa noted that Tuhoto Ariki was breathing fire and he tried to sound casual.

'Ariki, there you are, greetings priest.'

Ariki's tall, erect bearing gave the lie to his hundred years. His face was lean, the hawk-like nose turned down and the strong prominent cheek bones gave the Tohunga a stern, uncompromising look which would aptly describe the priest of Te Arawa. The grey eyes, uncharacteristic of his race, were set deeply in the hollows of their sockets. The gaze of the feared Tohunga could search the hearts of men and suck out their souls, casting them into eternal chasms of despair. Respect for the old man was driven more by an outright fear from his tribe, rather than friendship or love. They believed that the old man had magical qualities.

'He speaks to people that no one can see.'

The eyes were today full of serpents and the two dark brackets above them lifted briefly in a silent and dour acknowledgement of the Rangatira as he entered the meeting house. In contrast to the Tohunga, Keepa was admired and respected by the councillors present, for his statesman-like qualities and the many acts of kindness to his people. The usual buzz of conversation was stilled at the entrance of both men.

The gathering of village councillors waited for a formal prayer from the Tohunga that would begin the meeting. By the look of fury on the old man's face it became obvious that the traditional karakia was not forthcoming, not today. Ariki hardly needed to hold his hand up to speak, and in the sudden hush of the room he cast a sullen look in the direction of the Rangatira before settling on the assembly, waiting for the Tohunga to speak. His voice knifed through the room casting the minds of his reluctant audience into the gulf of uncertainty.

'When the pakeha first arrived I said that we should kick them out. Some of you present in this whare were not even alive at that time. So? Why have we not razed that abominable building to the ground?' It has defiled our tribe. The young men attend that place every night, drinking that which is tapu to us. Our people are being corrupted by the pakeha. The moment their feet touched the land it became defiled. Look at your wives and your daughters, wandering indolently around the village attired in what the foreign women call, a 'dress.' The cloth of the pakeha is an outrage. Worn by our women it takes away their dignity.'

The Tohunga's face contorted in his fury and his lean frame shook with rage as he continued. 'You have become the *Tautangata of the pakeha, blinded by their gold. Can you not see what is happening to our people?'

The look of disgust from the old man changed to a sneer of contempt. 'But of course you cannot answer the question. It is impossible for you to answer the question. You are the plaything of the pakeha, mesmerized by their money, their liquor and now it has come to this. That you prefer to get drunk every night, treat your women like slaves for your own foul pleasure. Where once this sacred earth drank the blood of warriors who would protect the whanau, it reeks now of your vomit. There!'

The index finger of the Tohunga clawed across the uneasy quiet, pointing in the direction of large building, standing to one side of the village, the hotel inn owned and built by the practical and ever affable, Mr. Joseph McRae. 'There is the cursed edifice of your pakeha friends. Let it burn…burn to the ground and kick out those who are not tangata whenua.'

'You talk nonsense old man. The Englishman has built the tavern *for* the foreign visitors. Now they can stay here, bathe in our pools, draw their pictures of Otukapuarangi and Te Tarata. For this they pay well. I tell you now the foreign money has brought much wealth to our…'

'Wealth? Wealth!' The old man's reply cut short the speaker's homily on riches. A gold coin had appeared in the priest's hand as though manifest out of the sullied ambience of the room, or, more realistically, the folds of his cloak. 'You call this piece of filth–*wealth!*' The cadaverous finger pointed across the imposing entrance of the meeting house, towards the bountiful frontiers of forest and lake that bounded their lands. 'And what is that outside if it is not wealth? Bestowed to us from the time when our great navigator, Tama-Te-Kapua himself, led us to this land.' He added judiciously, 'guided of course by the great Tohunga who had accompanied him on that first journey.' He flung the coin against one of the walls where the offending article bounced back and landed on the floor, untouched because the coin had become suddenly tapu.

'Pakeha money? You vile dogs! Pakeha, bootlickers. You Matiu, dare to question the Tohunga, to call my prophesy nonsense.'

Matiu Iorangi, the speaker and one of the council, was always a little uncomfortable when he looked into the face of Ariki the Tohunga. When the village priest was enraged, lines appeared on the Tohunga's forehead and face, as though an entity outside the world of men had attached its own malefic signature to the dynamic moko that had been inscribed on the priest's face, signifying his rank and his status within the tribe. The effect resembled that of a wild animal about to devour its prey.

Keepa, the Rangatira, had seen this animal in one of the picture books that belonged to Mr. McRae, owner of the offending tavern. The beast was called a tiger; it ate the flesh of wild beasts and of humans and a more ferocious animal he could not imagine. The old Tohunga was standing half in shadow, as enraged as he had ever seen him. The lines had suddenly appeared, as if by some dire alchemy, and he noted that some of the assembly standing near the man had moved to one side. Keepa, who had been silent during the old man's tirade, wondered if it had been foolish of Matiu Iorangi to refer the old man's speech about the pakehas as nonsense. He remembered what happened to Aporo, chief of the Ngati Hinemihi, a month ago, at a meeting similar to this but with a horrifying result, so he was relieved when Matio spoke again, this time in a more placatory tone.

'Your pardon Tohunga, I spoke of course, out of turn. As always you have the goodness of our people in your heart.'

It was as though the priest hadn't heard at all. His face had contorted into a funneled rage of fire and dust, eyes protruding out of the deep sockets, his mouth opening and closing in a fury as this time he spoke in an ancient tongue to the assembly, so that even the Rangatira, standing to one side of the gathering, understood only a few words of what the priest said. Words that Keepa understood to be messengers of maligned fate.

'You will find out....soon enough...sooner than you think...I have awakened the guardians from their eternal sleep and they have shown me a sight that will make your bones rattle in fear.' The old man, trembling in his anger, pointed vaguely in the direction outside the village. Some of the younger men in the council laughed, but their laughter bore no conviction, neither did it sound remotely like the laughter of joy or of mirth as the old man stormed out of the meeting house.

*

Keepa walked back alone to his whare, set to one side of the smaller houses and built partly of stone, which was the traditional dwelling of the tribal

10

chief. A thin moon peered over the horizon, becoming gradually fatter as it grew out of the hills that guarded Lake Tarawera. It lit up the lake, casting a trace of silver across the dark water, both removing and adding to its mystery, then touching the shore at one end. But the beauty of the rising moon, the silver fragmentation of the water and the two moreporks flying low over the lake escaped the troubled eyes of the tribal chief. Instead he saw only the face of fury as the old man walked out of the hall cursing the young men who laughed, cursing the elders who had called his ideas nonsense, then the entire village, sparing no one.

Keepa Te Rangipuawhe chief of the Arawa had seen anger in men before this. He was a tall man descended from a long line of tribal warrior chiefs, with an inherently noble bearing and stature. His head was large, the nose finely shaped, with a broad forehead and strong square-cut chin and ample head of jet hair. His mouth, relaxed and seemingly ready to smile, was fringed by a neat, spade-shaped beard. Usually he laughed inwardly at the foibles of men, but tonight his eyes overlooked the houses, the trees and the fields of corn planted by the pakeha. They searched across the great lake, finding in the darkness of approaching night the looming shadow of Mount Tarawera.

The Tohunga's rage had made the face of Tuhoto Ariki almost sub-human. The Rangatira did not think it fanciful when he thought the face at one point resembled the dynamic contortions of a mud pool in its fiery convolutions and eruptions. The wrath of Tuhoto Ariki was far removed from that of ordinary men. It was a supernatural energy, capable of awakening unknown, malefic forces that existed within the universe. A power, he reasoned, that was either creative or destructive in its consequence. His influence reached out into the ether assailing the palpable things of the earth, and if he did not fear the Tohunga's fire, it definitely made him apprehensive.

When the Tohunga had stormed out of the meeting place he was still listening, and it was he alone of all his tribe who, instead of joining in with their hollow laughter, had caught the man's words. Ariki had said, *'orange rain...destruction...'* and he had caught the final words *'...the mountain...will speak...'*

FOUR

Keepa noted the empty space inside the dwelling of the Tohunga. Two young men standing outside the whare had claimed to see him leave earlier.

'And you saw him leave? When was that?'

'Early morning, Rangatira. He walked off in that direction.' The man pointed to the lake. 'We asked him where he was going.'

The Rangatira, knowing Ariki's present mood and his habit of sullen reticence, didn't expect much from the two young men. 'I don't suppose he said anything.'

'Actually he did Sir.'

'Well, surprising. What did he say?'

'The mountain.'

'What about the mountain?'

'Sir, he said he was going up the mountain.'

'The Mountain?'

'Tarawera.'

The young men looked uncomfortable, sensing the change of mood in the Rangatira.

'Are you sure you heard correctly?'

The other man who hadn't spoken added. 'He wasn't in the best of moods, Rangatira. He walked off saying something about hell and fire. Sometimes you can't understand his words.'

'Yes, I know.'

'Sir, the last we saw of him he was heading towards the lake.'

'All right.' Keepa left them and walked in the direction of the hotel at one end of the village.

He agreed with the priest about the young men's drinking habits but you could hardly blame McRae for that or indeed any of the visitors from foreign lands. They came from a long distance, paid good money and left, happy with what they had seen. If the men drank and misbehaved themselves that was their own lookout. He had discussed the business with the proprietor and McRae had confessed that he too was uncomfortable with the revelry that went on. He would have to think long and hard about a solution and it would have to involve the elders.

Tuhoto's sudden decision to visit the mountain for some reason nagged at the back of his mind. One thing was certain, it was impossible for the centenarian to get anywhere near the top, wasn't it? There was much that he did not know about the Tohunga. He and everyone else for that matter.

FIVE

At the far end of Lake Tarawera a rising sun lanced the still water into jagged orange and crimson, scattering thin wisps of cloud as it ascended in its preordained passage over the watery horizon.

Ariki studied the sunrise, standing in silence next to the ferryman. He motioned with his hand that he was ready. The ferryman let the Tohunga get in the canoe then gently pushed the small, smoothly-shaped boat into the water. Helping him was out of the question. He asked the priest if he wished to sit but the old man rejected the offer and stood at the prow. The well-muscled shoulders and arms of Rapata drove the boat smoothly towards their destination. The old man had simply pointed in the direction of Mount Tarawera, its giant image reflected in the lake, and that was all. By custom, he never spoke to the high priest. He had occasionally taken him across the lake to visit dwellings at the far end and only spoke to him when asked. Sometimes the Tohunga stayed longer, performing a ceremony that might take two or three days. He knew that the Tohunga was over a hundred years in age, yet people feared him more than ever.

The priest was wearing his ceremonial cloak this morning, the brown and white feathers slightly damp from the mist rising off the water. Rapata wondered what was happening today but that was something he daren't ask a man of such high rank. They sped across the glassy water for about fifteen minutes. It was not unusual to see patches of vapour hovering across the lake on a clear day, usually it would be early in the morning. The ferryman noticed that a mist had thickened to one side of the lake, almost like a cloud that had descended on the water's surface, its form changed into a substance resembling a slabby, corporeal gruel drifting across the water, coming closer until it had enveloped them, and for a moment he lost direction.

Rapata felt suddenly depressed, staring ahead and around him into the nothingness of grey, damp matter. For a moment he had no idea where they were, then something to their left, massive, moving towards them, a dark shape coming out of the miasma. What he saw next made him stop paddling. His body shook as though with the onset of an ague, the muscled arms suddenly slack. The ferryman looked down, hoping that his eyes had betrayed him, that he would open them again and see only the open lake.

The prow of a war canoe, a waka taua of ancient design, emerged out of the mist and to his horror was heading straight for his boat. The occupants of the war-ship were looking directly ahead, as though the ferryman and his passenger did not exist. At one end, unmistakable in his chieftain's cloak of feathers and his moko, holding a huge spear, the man's eyes were prominent dark holes that were fixed on the far horizon. The men in the waka taua had stopped paddling in perfect unison, their oars held aloft as though in salute or recognition of something, some event that had or had not yet happened. A collision was imminent, the razor-sharp prow of the war-canoe would knife through them in its headlong passage and Rapata knew that both he and the Tohunga were about to die. Terror released the torpor in his muscles, and gripping the oar he plunged the instrument into the water about to drive them forward.

Ariki was looking intently at the war craft and his directive, spoken with absolute authority, cut through the sepulchral fog. 'Stay where you are.'

It was as though, for the silent occupants of the ancient te-waka, Rapata and the Tohunga did not exist.

He braced himself and the dark shape came onto them but there was no collision, no splintering of timbers, no broken bodies floundering in the lake as the long dark shape passed *through them,* its aerodynamic prow heading towards Tarawera mountain.

Matter merged with illusion and it became impossible to tell which was which, only that Rapata felt himself aware and unaware, liquified into a cosmic field far removed from what he had deemed as his palpable world of substance. He had gone beyond fear, hope, love, hate. Beyond the petty foibles of humanity, and there was only, for this moment in time, the ordinance of being.

Rapata's hands and shoulders seemed frozen. In their owner's state of terror they had lost all volition. He tried his best to move his own vessel but he found it impossible to lift his arms into position to grip the paddle and drive the boat forward and away, as far as possible from this nightmare.

17

The ancient craft had stopped. For the moment, its cutwater prow pointed directly at the mountain, and now Rapata received his second shock. The men in the phantom canoe had turned and were facing the Tohunga. The warrior faces were changing, the flesh was rapidly peeling away so that they appeared lean, cadaverous. A rapid metamorphosis was taking place within the muscular bodies until the ferryman was staring at a giant canoe driven by a skeleton crew. Despite the heavy miasma that surrounded them, the eyes appeared to have a luminous quality, prominent through the skulls, observing Rapata, seeing him, seeing through him, the teeth in a fixed rictus, impossible for a terrestrial to look at, or rationalize, and he turned his face staring down into the water at his own tepid image, powerless to countenance the vile, undead vapours of the insubstantial entities, masked in human form. God!...God! Why…what had possessed him this day to ferry the Tohunga across this cursed place? Rapata's body had gone ice cold and he thought he was going to faint. He felt a compulsion to lift his head, and when he looked up the vessel with its crew of dead warriors had disappeared.

For the first time since they had started their journey, Ariki turned and looked at him, taking in the terror of the ferryman, his face unaccountably kind, understanding the young man's horror.

'Stow your paddle Rapata, there is no need for you to row.'

He could not understand the priest's instruction, issued with calm authority. Neither was he prepared to ask, his throat numb with shock, fully accepting the command of the man standing at the prow whose powers would convene the etheric world onto the lake and into their presence. Were they just going to stay here in the middle of Lake Tarawera, to do what? Then he felt the surge of his boat, heard the familiar hiss of his canoe as it drove through the water, towards the mountain that seemingly waited for its occupants.

Ariki, a half smile in his face, stood with both arms folded in front of his chest. He had wrapped the ceremonial cloak across his body as they sped through the water, caught up in the wake of the ancient war canoe driven by dead warriors. It seemed as though they were travelling too fast; they would reach the sandy shore of the mountain in a tenth of the time it would have taken him to row. Rapata felt a cold wind and looking up he noted the Tohunga's cloak, tight across the thin, wiry body, the ends flapping in the air-stream.

The small boat slid across the lake for about twenty minutes and then he saw the steep banks of the mountain coming up. He tried to brake with his paddle but it was impossible and he knew they would crash into the bank.

Ariki lifted his right hand towards his shoulder, moving it slowly, patiently downwards, and the small canoe began to slow down until it stopped in shallow water, not far from the sandy beach that fringed the edge of Mount Tarawera. He turned away from the shoreline and looked at Rapata, seeing in his young face the residue of delayed shock and fear, the skin pale and cold to the touch, with droplets of moisture on his face, not from the lake. The priest seemed amused as he studied him for a moment, then he spoke.

'All right, you can rest, boy. What you have seen is not for the eyes of others. They were spectres, ghosts of men, of warriors long gone to their place of rest. This is as it should be and their appearance is a warning of what I am about to do. You are not to speak of this, not to anyone. Now take me to shore. Wait here until my return.'

Calmed and reassured by the Tohunga's words he was about to suggest that for the hundred year old man to walk to the top of the mountain and back, apart from being impossible, would take all day and all night but after what he had seen, the dimensions of his world had changed.

'Yes, of course Sir,' he said and sat still.

The priest looked directly at him. The bones protruding at his age, working their way through the flesh. The eyes were glowing as though in revelation. The thick bushy eyebrows lifted as he studied the young man then, for the first time that he or anyone had seen such a gesture in the Tohunga, the thin lips of the old man parted across the mouth forming a rare smile.

'Yes, good.....but now you need to get us there.' He pointed, still smiling, in the direction of the sandy beach, some twenty metres in front of them.

SIX

One month earlier.

Aporo Te-Wharekaniwha, chief of the Ngati Hinemihi, stood outside the tribal meeting house. He had been asked to pose for photographs directly in front of the imposing entrance, visited today by the elders of his tribe and the pakeha tourists who came from lands so remote he could not picture them in his mind. It was a pity that the Rangatira, Keepa Te Rangipuawhe, could not attend this particular gathering. There were about fifteen people who were to be shown inside the structure, replete with its historic carvings, and before their entry the Tohunga would perform his ritual to remove any tapu associated by the presence of pakeha.

The Tohunga present today was Tuhoto Ariki, high priest of the Tuhorangi and Ngati Hinemihi tribes and a direct descendant of the Te Arawa. Aporo was uncomfortable with the old man's presence, but it was a requirement for him to be present during important meetings.

Tuhoto had arrived with a scowl on his face and during the ritual Aporo could see him getting more and more irritated. At one point he stopped, looked around at the carvings of tribal gods and spat on the ground in a temper, his utterance interrupting the sacred ritual that only he could perform. His voice rasped uncomfortably across the room. 'The tapu in this place is already broken so what I am doing here is absolutely futile. It has no meaning whatsoever.' The old man ended his ceremony in a hurry and stood to one side of the whare, unnoticed by the tour group.

Meanwhile, the large bulk of the Rangatira had been joined by some of the elders, his wife on one side. The chief was happy to oblige when a visitor asked him to hold the greenstone adze aloft, in the manner of a warrior.

Kanu, his personal interpreter, translated, explaining in his animated and occasionally unintelligible English the lineage of his tribe and the ancient history of the gods. Aporo was especially pleased when Kanu told them about the power of the chief in Maoridom. Dressed in the ceremonial and sacred robe of a chieftain, he waved the adze above his head, one arm stretched out to attack the invisible enemy.

Apart from his status, the money was an added treasure. The ancient carvings of the deities inside the meeting house had been thanked personally by him and he asked a local man to remove the traditional paua shells that made up the omniscient eyes of the gods, replacing them with gold coins from the pakeha. This he did to please his gods and members of the council, regardless of the rumblings of discontent from Tuhoto.

Aporo re-entered the whare along with some of the tribe's high ranking councillors, after the pakeha tourists had gone. At no point did the old man call him a fool but his actions and the way the Tohunga was speaking to him in front of his tribe was insulting to the chief of the Ngati Hinemihi, who believed in his own infallibility concerning the governance of his tribe.

The old man's hand shook in fury as he indicated the ancient carvings that encompassed the walls, the traditional and sacred paua shell removed from the eye sockets and replaced with what, to the priest, were worthless bits of tin. 'You! You are entirely responsible for this. How many times do I have to tell you?'

He pointed to the carvings positioned along the walls and the supporting beams of the roof, carved extensively with images of Tane, Maui, Rangi, deities over whom the Tohunga had performed the karakia that rendered each entity sacred and inviolate to the tribe.

'What is this doing here? And this and this and this?' The old man stood with his face closer than any other man or woman of Te Arawa would dare against a chief and tribal leader. 'Damn you! Your greed has defiled the sacred rites and you have debased yourself before my people.'

'Your people! And when was that? Who is the head of this tribe? Who led us into war against the forces of Te Kooti? Who burnt their canoes and slaughtered them like dogs?'

'Led...led...led?' You stood at the back and it was the warriors of the tribe who did that. *I* blessed them. *I* told them to win the war and it was *my* curse upon the invaders from the north that defeated them.'

'Be careful you old fool. You are crossing the boundaries of my authority.'

'It is *you* who needs to take care. Authority, is it, Aporo Te Wharekaniwha? Authority to do what? Debauch with the pakeha, drink until our so-called warriors cannot stand, cannot speak? Your authority has long since vanished into the wind. Lift your head up to heaven my friend, you'll see no god, only your own vanity.'

In his anger the chief had become suddenly aware of the elders of his tribe who stood, amazed and embarrassed, as they witnessed the argument of the Tohunga and the tribal leader and he tried once more to regain his authority.

'Stop this. Stop it at once!'

'Stop? Ha! I have not even begun.'

'You vicious old fool.'

'You vile dog you ....'

The big man had turned to the side as though to deflect the wrath of the old man. When he turned the face of the Tohunga was before him, snarling, twisted in its rage. But now Aporo had lost his senses and, unable to stop himself, he struck the Tohunga fully across the old, leathery face.

The slap was delivered on the instant: without thought, without taking into account the consequences of the aftermath. The sound of it, sharp and distressing, was the prelude to a dreadful silence, far worse than the vituperative argument that had preceded the action.

It occurred to Aporo then, on the instant, that he should go down on his knees, touch the Tohunga's feet, begging his pardon, saying that it was his temper that got the better of him and ask humbly for

24

forgiveness, but his legs had turned to stone, his face rigid in fear and apprehension and, in any case, his innate pride got the better of him and he was unable to do these things. For a moment he glanced down at his hand as though it alone had been responsible for this action.

The room had gone still, like a picture suddenly frozen in time. To the fifty or so people in the meeting house the sound of the slap was the harbinger of things to come. Something infinitely horrible, portending death and destruction. Would *they* be to blame, they who had witnessed this absolute blasphemy? What would the Tohunga do now? The room had on the instant changed into a space that housed statues, each face sculpted in horror and disbelief, coupled to a fervent wish that they were not here today, that this had not happened, not in *their* presence, not at any time.

Ariki had stood still as he received the slap, his face unnaturally calm, the eyes absolutely aware of the moment, attentive of the awful punishment that would follow this the most fundamental of all crimes in Maoridom, the striking of a Tohunga in public– the reverberation of its dreadful note echoing across the chasm of the cosmic field, piercing the fabric of eternity as its strident note battered the gates of hell, shrieking for vengeance.

For agonised moment after moment they heard the old man speak a lengthy incantation in a language so ancient that not a man understood his words, and if they did it was mere fragments, messengers of death, eternal anguish and, as though for the first time, they knew his awesome power, knew it to the very core of their beings. In the indeterminable silence of the room, unattended by their gods, they could hear only the sullen canticle of black angels approaching, a divine justice beyond their scope as warriors, as protectors of the whenua to defend, or as mortals to countenance.

The old man was laughing. His laughter flailed the men present in the room, like jagged stones flung into their heads, echoing and ricocheting across their meeting house. The discordant notes whirled across the walls, the statues, the sacred relics inside the ceremonial room as Ariki pointed to the images of Maui, then to the lesser gods in the room.

The offending coins that had recently been placed meticulously inside the eyes of the deities started to fall out, some with force, striking one or two of the men who moved rapidly out of the way in case the tapu should reach them. Then all the coins began to burst out of the sockets, landing with a hard clatter on the stone floor until the eyes of the gods were sightless and it was only the awesome wrath in the eyes of the prophet that stared into the past and saw the future at one and the same time.

The voice of Ariki was suddenly calm, logical, the words infinitely more dangerous than his previous rant at the chief. 'For this hara, Te Wharekaniwha, I, the high priest of the Tuhorangi tribe and a descendant of the ancient Tohungas of Te Arawa, place at this moment of time, a kanga upon you. I, who alone of all the tribes of all the Te Arawa and all of the Tuhorangi, have the power of makutu, place my curse upon your head.'

The assembly were facing the Priest who had walked some distance from the gathering, standing now close to the ancient carving of Maui, his whole concentration focused upon Aporo.

'Look all of you, here, assembled in this sacred place, defiled by the man to whom the gods had granted their authority. He who stands here day upon day, posturing vainly, spear in one hand, axe in the other and in his heart nothing other than a false pride. Aporo Te Kaniwha– a matae atua will descend upon your body and your spirit. In sleep you will have no sanctuary from your vile dreams of loss, of horror and desertion. In death you will continue to exist, alone, confused, condemned to wander the region of the undead, the land of shadows. Lost, Aporo Te Wharekaniwha, lost for all time. As I have spoken, it will be. Tonight, when you awaken, the demon will already have possessed you in its merciless clutch, to the very core of your being.'

He paused for a moment and stared hard at the men; warriors, guides, leaders and artisans who had built the tribe. Not one of them, not the warriors, not the men of high rank, could countenance that look and they stared at their feet, their bodies robbed for the moment of all volition. In their state of terror Ariki spoke again, his words portends of an avenging angel.

'Now let me tell you, even that will be as nothing to what will come.'

There had been no shouting, no rending of curses, no calling of names shouted out across the room. Ostensibly not even a show of anger by the Tohunga and that was what terrified them most of all. It was as if what he spoke had been written in the memory of the past and its promulgation with such deadly matter-of-fact certainty was unassailable. The punishment had therefore nothing to do with the man's vengeance; the procedure was inscribed in the tenets of Maoridom. Strike a priest–pay the price.

They looked at the tribal chief and his face was as whey. But he was the leader and he, Aporo, forced some semblance of a laugh, trying his best to put on a brave front, his lips parting in a distorted grimace that was a poor attempt for a smile as he looked around the room, seeing the insipid faces of his councillors.

'Ha! Words, words, words. Your language is as the wind that passes over our heads and it is without meaning. Your precious kanga shall pass and dissolve into nothing.' But his voice was weak, the final words lost in his fear of the absolute curse uttered by the man most feared by his tribe.

The meeting, assembled in perfect order, fragmented now in wonderful disarray, with no ceremonial greetings, no farewells as they fled out into the night.

*

Wiremu Tamati, a respected councillor of Wairoa and a good friend of Aporo Te Wharekaniwha, met with the tribal chief standing just outside his whare. Aporo stared at the great lake as the moon was ascending out of the water, casting a silver pathway across its length. The man turned, seeing Wiremu approaching.

'So, Wiremu. What do you think?'

'Think?'

'The business of the meeting, of course it was never brought up. You know, a new drain to be put outside the whares to keep us dry in winter, the pakeha...'

Wiremu listened politely to the chief's words that he knew were a cover up for what really happened, the real 'business' of the meeting. He let the chief finish before he spoke.

'Well frankly, Aporo, I can't even think straight after all that.'

'Oh...you mean the old man letting off steam?' He tried a laugh, this one an improvement on the attempt inside the meeting house. 'Believe all that and you believe anyt...anything.'

Wiremu said nothing, but his breath escaping slowly through clenched teeth made a hissing sound in the still air. 'Aporo, what you did was inexcusable! Think of the danger you may well have brought upon yourself. I fear for you Aporo, for your family.'

At his words the chief's bluster seemed to dissolve. 'Well yes. Of course I wish...I wish I hadn't but...sometimes we speak in anger. His curse. Terrible...terrible. Does he really have the power Wiremu? Will it happen as he says?'

'I do not know.' Wiremu was about to add, yes I think so, but changed that to, 'well that's what we are led to believe. You must admit that his performance in there was impressive, to say the least. I am not sure, who can be certain, but I do know that his power is very great.'

'I have heard this also. Some say the most ill-tempered man and yet he holds the power of life and death over us all. Is there anything, anyway that it is possible… to remove…'

Remove the curse?' So I have heard from a former Tohunga. I don't remember his name but he says categorically that if a man dies before the ordained time the curse will not follow him after death.'

'In other words…'

'In other words should you die now, or tonight, before the curse takes hold, the kanga cannot work because your spirit is not there to receive it.'

'So I kill myself before the moon reaches its fullest ascension. I die, but the curse does not follow me into my afterlife. Nice choice, Wiremu!'

'Well, that's what I heard.' He added, smiling in jest to ease Aporo's fear. 'Seems like you haven't much of a choice.'

A flight of birds landed on the water, breaking the silence.

'Perhaps the old man is a fraud. Remember, he has to look good to the others.'

Wharekaniwha looked out across the moonlit waters of the lake and shook his head as though to dispel thoughts of the events that had taken place. 'We'll see,' was all he said and they changed the subject, talking of other things before Wiremu left.

The Chief stood for some time outside the whare, seeing events far removed from the stretch of water directly in front of him. Despite Wiremu's suggestion that the old man could be all bluff and bluster he felt a sudden chill in his bones. He was a warrior, so why should he fear a tetchy old man? Progress had come to his people and to his village. The old man had no right to stop progress, none at all. As for this business of placing the kanga upon his head, this was just not acceptable. That's right! He would simply not *accept* the curse of the Tohunga. To hell with it all.

Over the horizon the moon had cast a silver stream of light and a thin wind ruffled the waters so that it moved in a series of wavy lines across Lake Tarawera almost as though the silvery shaft was approaching where he stood. Satisfied that the whole silly business was a thing that had come and gone, Aporo retired into his dwelling and slept almost immediately.

*

The moon cast a sliver of silver into the room and across the face of the sleeper. The light slanting across his eyes awakened Aporo. He remembered the conflict with the Tohunga and wave of fear swept through his body. Like many or all of his tribe, what happened after death was of concern to him.

It served no purpose lying in his bed in torment, so he got up and moved outside the whare. The moon had passed over the water, which by contrast seemed as a dark shadow against the land. He was alone; his tribe the Ngati Hinemihi asleep in their beds, and it was long hours to daybreak.

'A Matae atua will descend upon your body and your spirit.'

'My god, Wharekaniwha, what you did was inexcusable man!'

The words flung through the night air, like the jagged clatter of coins inside the whare, assailing his mind, and he felt his agony seeping and pulsing through his body, his soul.

...should you die now or tonight, before the curse takes hold, the curse cannot work because your spirit is not there to receive it.'

Yes, of course. Should I die tonight. Should he die. Dying was easy compared to his existence in an endless world of shadows. Leave his young wife, his tribe, the elders, and the wealth he had amassed through his efforts. He was the chief, leader, and despite what the old man had said, highly respected.

...you will wander the regions of the undead. Lost Te Wharekaniwha, lost for all time.

The thought came to him. A solution, a final solution for himself. His throat had gone dry with fear, its unseen, unwanted texture coursed through Aporo's muscled frame, pulsing through his blood. Without thinking he suddenly fled into the whare and saw the green adze lying where he had slept. Picking up the weapon, he moved to one side of the room, breathing in short gasps of fear as he held it in both hands, lined up with his face. He knew of a warrior, shamed for his cowardice, who split his skull open with one quick, decisive blow to his head. His grip on the handle tightened, he moved his hand away from his body so there was just enough distance to strike, hard...fast, one decisive blow to end it all. To elude the curse in the afterlife. The sleep of death–without the afterlife. The adze was used for show now, but its edge on the hard smooth greenstone was razor sharp. One blow...to die now...die now ...die now...die...die...die.

His arms shook with the agony then he lowered both his hands, gripped hard and brought the instrument of death up with both hands at speed and – stopped. An inch away from his head, from the centre of his skull, and he knew it was impossible for him to do this thing.

A sweat had broken out over his arms and face and was running down his neck. He walked out into the night again, having placed his adze where it belonged, its smooth handle wet from his agony. The night was cool, somewhere a morepork shrieked into the latticed shadows of the nikau palms, and he heard the voice of Wiremu, the voice of sweet reason.

Look! Perhaps the old man is a fraud. Remember, he has to look good to the others.'

Te Wharekaniwha felt his strength of body and of his spirit returning, banishing forever the vile substance of his fear. Ha! So what if the spirits of the dark world tormented him? He, chieftain of Ngati Hinemihi, would torment them far worse than they could imagine.

Above his head the city of stars flickered anxiously, lest their beauty should be obscured by cloud threatening the horizon.

SEVEN

The ferryman had seen a hundred-year-old man begin his ascent and prepared himself for a long wait. The Tohunga had walked a few steps towards some dense undergrowth of wild flax and fern. Sometimes, when he ferried the pakeha visitors who wanted to visit the mountain, they would choose this path, and he would see them clearly as they emerged through dense flax bush onto the hard grassy stretch which was as far as they were allowed. No one as yet, apart from a missionary in the early days of his tribe, had ever scaled to the top. It was of course regarded as tapu for his people to ascend the mountain and he had not seen the priest emerge onto the clear section before his walk to the summit.

After what he had experienced on the lake this morning his view of the holy man had changed altogether. He had always respected the priest, accepting without reservation the Tohunga's anger over the tribe's greed for pakeha liquor and their money. A view not shared by many of the younger men of his tribe who had no respect for him but feared him enough to keep out of his way. Neither did Rapata see him as just a tetchy old man. What had happened this morning was an event that did not belong here, was not of this earth. He saw Tuhoto now as a man with vast power. A man? Was he even that or was he…what was he? He became confused and if he could articulate his thoughts he would have called him an entity, a metaphysical apparition yet palpable in body, a visitor to the Arawa, to ensure tribal discipline and removal of strangers that were polluting and defiling the land on which he and his ancestors had trod for centuries.

This place was a gift from the gods. Had not the navigator, the great Kupé, been guided by the spirits to a white cloud that stretched across the sea? What they found was different to anywhere that they had come across in their years of navigating the vast oceans, their long ships battered by storm, their timbers hammered against the ocean's watery anvil.

The story had it that the tribe in their long boats were about to pass and he had told them to head for the cloud. It shone in the sun, distant, pure in its whiteness, seeming to call them and the lead vessel cut through the ocean, followed by the small fleet, powered by the arms of his oarsmen. Kupé had told them that this was land to build a nation; that he would call it that land which, shrouded in mist, had been revealed to him and his descendants, so he called it, 'Aotearoa,' and thus it had come about.

Who else but Tuhoto Ariki could summon dead warriors, a dead Rangatira, at the helm of an ancient waka taua to cross the lake? He had felt the wind of the long boat as it passed through his small craft and there was the smell. Had it come from their bodies, from the ancient canoe? Burning smoke and the vile smell of burnt and rotting corpses. Only for a moment, then it had passed and he had felt his strength turn to water, weak almost as though he was about to faint. Ariki had his back turned to him, his attention on the

Waka Tua and its spectral occupants. Anticipating his terror, the priest had moved his hand in a gesture as though to say, 'be patient, it will pass.' He thought it had gone, seeing it fade across the lake, back to the place that existed beyond the frontier of his or his tribe's understanding, until he felt his own small craft heading towards the mountain.

Had the ferryman seen Tuhoto's progression towards the summit, transported on the shoulders of spectral warriors, the fainting fit would have taken hold again and without the priest's guiding power he would have entered an area of darkness, perhaps never to return. Hidden from human eyes, the Priest waited to one side of a clump of flax bushes as the spectral occupants of the war canoe that had taken on substance emerged from the lake and eased silently onto the sand. They paused for a moment, awaiting their Rangatira's signal with the dispassionate faces of warriors long absent from the human stage, until the Tohunga's call had resonated across the quantum field to attend his sacrament, and they had arrived, in perfect order of unison, across the frontiers of infinity.

Tuhoto was lifted upon the shoulders of two warriors and carried towards the top of Mount Tarawera where his whispers of vengeance, of justice, would be received into the gaping mouth of the caldera. His silent attendants moved away from him, as though what would happen next was only for the Tohunga.

The priest had been here before. At that time not one of his tribe had been born. He had just turned twenty when he ascended to the peak and walked to the lip of the caldera. Looking into the depth of the mountain he had seen the giant sitting on a flat boulder with steam issuing from vents in the black earth. It was then that he had his first conversation with Tamahoi. As yet the mythical giant was unable to approach or to emerge onto the surface. He explained his story to the young Tohunga and told him that only a priest of great power could release him from his enforced confinement and that would be to unleash his powers across the land at the express order of such a person.

The detached eyes of Tamahoi recognised the priest, staring into the gaping mouth of Tarawera mountain. In the heat waves rising from the attendant fires below, the Tohunga's body seemed to quiver, becoming for moments at a time almost translucent, appearing to lack substance like the spectres behind him. His body began to glisten with water that seeped from him, and the guardian that had lived within the mountain for a thousand years knew that his tenure of exile had ended as the Tohunga incanted the kanga from the ancient tongue of his ancestors.

'The earth has become polluted with the feet of many pakeha.

My people have lost their innocence and greed has polluted their minds.

Your fire must purify the land and cleanse the infection.

Otukapuarangi, and Te Tarata shall drown in the waters of the lake.

I invest you now with the power of my authority, thus you are freed from your banishment.

37

Release the dogs of destruction and let your voice be heard across the earth and your fires reduce to ash the greed that has poisoned my land.'

For a moment there was silence, stillness.

The sound of distant thunder rose from deep within the mountain, the ground shook for a few moments then it was over and the Tohunga's charm was cast in the place that for the tribe had been absolutely tapu.

*

The ferryman waited for what in his reckoning would have been about forty minutes at the most, when he saw Ariki moving slowly down the slope and towards his canoe. He waited for the old man to settle in front of the vessel. He saw the spectral warriors, splendidly noble and correct, as they took up their positions in the war ship. They turned in perfect unity and held the long paddles like weapons in what he recognized was a final salute. The long boat slid outwards before they vanished to return from whence they came, and what had appeared as substance departed into the ether.

Rapata's fear had diminished, perhaps owing to the presence of the Tohunga, yet he was amazed by what he had seen, accepting why this hundred-year-old man had gone up and down a mountain much faster than it would have taken a warrior. The mountain was absolutely tapu and only Ariki could go there.

He would never speak of this to anyone. What he had seen would stay with him until his death. He sat down and turned the boat round until the canoe drifted away from the sandy edge of Tarawera.

Ariki spoke, his tone seemingly casual, matter-of-fact. 'Rapata, you will have to leave this place. Leave today. In three days from now you must be far from here. Go to Rotorua, and if you can, further. Do not come back–ever.'

The ferryman looked towards Ariki, nodded then turned and took the canoe slowly away from the mountain towards home, towards the sanctuary of Te Wairoa. Towards sweet reason.

Yes, he would without question follow the great Tohunga's advice. When Ariki spoke like this it was a personal message and to one as humble as himself, a compliment of the highest order, so he would leave, but there was something he had to do first. Something so important that he would not be able to go without doing this. As soon as he arrived he would go to the dwelling of Hunapo.

EIGHT

One month earlier.

Aporo Te Wharekaniwha woke early the next morning to the familiar call of birdsong that drifted across the forests. As always he walked to the lake and bathed before taking his breakfast, his best meal of the day. He had forgotten completely the events of the previous night and when they came to mind as he washed his bulk in the cool water of the lake, they seemed to matter not at all. As for getting up in the dead of night and all that ridiculous business with the adze, in his mind now it was an absolute nonsense. What a fool he was to think, to even imagine for an instant, that the old man had any power over a supreme chief of Ngati Hinemihi.

Walking back to his whare he smiled and greeted the early risers of his village. There were not as many as there used to be. The laggers had been doing the usual drinking and goings on at the tavern, and so what? Young men, warriors, had to let off steam once in a while. They would soon perform another dance with their weapons if called upon to defend their people. Things were going well and there was no need for war, for battle. So let them have their fun. Money was flowing in and he would soon replace the gold coins in the eyes of the carvings. That ridiculous performance last night with the coins popping out. A cheap magician's trick no doubt, practiced for hours by the old man. Well, as things got better and better, the rest of the elders would soon realise what a fraud he was. Yes, life was good. That business of last night. Amazing how the old fool had got to him.

In the distance he saw Wiremu come over for breakfast. Wiremu usually saw him in the mornings. The tempting aromas of his wife's cooking more often than not led him in this direction. Poor Wiremu's wife, his lovely Petani, had passed away one year ago.

Wiremu greeted Aporo, as his wife, helped by her daughters, called them over. This morning it was the roasted pork baked in the earth's furnace from the previous night, and a heap of vegetables, which always included fresh, wild puha. The new mill ground the wheat that had been recently introduced into their diet, and the pakehas had shown the tribe how to cook and make bread. The food was adopted with enthusiasm by some of his people who by now could make it better than the pakeha.

'Come on Wiremu, dig in brother. We're going to have a full house today, I can sense it.'

'Well you look a lot brighter than you did last night, Aporo. Good thing too. Told you the old fellow was all wind and no substance. Ah! But this is the life, pass that pork over, yes my friend with the bread. Man, this is good food!'

'And all my wife's cooking Wiremu.'

Absolutely friend.' Wiremu acknowledged the lady who was eating along with her daughters to one side of the whare. 'And, as always, I thank you for this, Ngareta. My beautiful Petani will bless you wherever she is.'

'You are always welcome Wiremu, with no one to cook for you now that your Petani has gone. Take some pork home for later.'

*

It happened within the space of two hours while the chief was walking along the road that led to the tavern. At first he thought it was something in the meat, maybe it had gone bad. A cold sweat came over his body and he knew he was about to lose his food. He was hardly able to walk, and having evacuated his breakfast in a nearby field he had to struggle back home to recover. His family were probably having the same problem and he wondered what had gone wrong with the pork

Their two daughters were tidying up and he heard his wife singing at the back of the house. They were surprised to see him looking pale but he was irritated with them for making a fuss. 'Stop your nonsense! I'll be fine in a few minutes, I always eat too much, that's all your good cooking,' he joked. Wonder where Wiremu is, poor chap.

*

The illness took hold gradually. At first he found that he could eat small amounts of food, taken with water. Any pakeha liqueur from the tavern was out of the question, McRae's advice when he managed a walk to the tavern the next day. This time he went along with Wiremu, who had not been affected at all by the 'bad pork' He hung on to that notion. In his mind it was obvious that had caused his illness. It was a large leg of wild pork and obviously one part of the meat had gone bad.

'In no time at all, Mr McRae, in no time at all I will recover.'

'Well, of course, yes a big fellow like you. But do be advised and take the tablets I gave you, Chief Aporo. Three a day with a little water. Oh, by the way I heard a strange rumour, about the so-called curse by that old feller. Don't believe a word of it.' He laughed out loud. 'Pakeha medicine will fix you up, rest assured my friend.' He was about to say pakeha medicine is stronger than any curse from the old Tohunga but was glad he didn't. The chief's friend Wiremu, who was with him today, had turned away to speak to someone at the bar. McRae noted that he might have been trying to hide the look of fear and disbelief on his face when he talked about the Tohunga and pakeha medicine.

Within a week, Te Wharekaniwha was able only to walk for short periods at a time. He said that he didn't actually feel ill, not as such. It was just that he could not eat food, at all. He would walk to the table in his whare, the table was a mark of his high rank in the village, but it became impossible to look at the food for long. It was as though the food was to his mind not food at all. It could have been any substance and it had no place inside his body. Water was not enough, and his massive strength was diminishing fast so he had to lie down for long periods, day and night.

*

Wiremu was inside the tavern, sitting at one of the small tables placed there for guests. Only pakeha and Maori of high rank could actually sit at the table provided by the proprietor. McRae came over and offered the elder another beer. Wiremu usually was very circumspect with drinking. He had seen the drunken orgies that took place with the so called 'shows,' put on by the younger men and women of his tribe. At first they were well organised hakas, singing and dances, something to be proud of. Within a few months they had degenerated into shameful nonsense. Drunken pakehas were also to blame but that was no excuse. His wife had died a year ago. He missed her and was not prepared to sink her memory into an alcoholic haze. In any case he felt it would be undignified for him, as an elder, to drink to that extent. McRae presumed Wiremu's silence meant consent and pushed a small glass of beer in front of him then asked him how his friend the chief was getting on.

'Not so well, unfortunately, he can't seem to eat.' Wiremu was implying that Te-Wharekaniwha was unable to eat at all, that the sight of food did nothing for him. The proprietor assumed that because the chief was so sick he couldn't stomach food. 'Well, didn't the tablets I gave him help at all? They're meant to make you well enough to eat.'

'It's not that, he just *can't* eat. I am not sure what has happened because I myself cannot identify it. As soon as he sees the food he walks away.'

'You mean that he doesn't want it, that it nauseates him?'

'No. He sees the food alright. It...it is as though he simply cannot *accept* that he should eat it. I see his face, it is, how can I put it? Without expression, as though what is there, does not exist. Or that it is simply not for him. I cannot explain it any other way.'

'Mm! That's different, that's not good at all. Sounds like some illness inside his head, wouldn't you say?'

'Indeed Mr. McRae. That's exactly it. Inside his head. It's driving his poor wife mad. She cooks the most delicious food but it is not the food, it is as you say some disturbance in the mind of Aporo, a strange illness that I have not seen before.'

McRae thought he would sound the Maori elder out, regarding the rumour he had gleaned from one of the tribe who was reluctant to say too much other than that Aporo Te Wharekaniwha had clashed with the old Tohunga, Tuhoto Ariki. 'I heard from someone that some magic, if that is the word, was used on him, some trouble between him and the old Tohunga. Of course you don't have to tell...'

'No, no, it's fine I can tell you now. Yes I was there, right there, when it happened. The two of them had a big disagreement about the ...' Wiremu went on to relate the entire story as it played out at the meeting. 'Yes, so after that things have got worse and worse. I told him at the time he should never have struck the Tohunga. It's something you don't do, and I do not think anyone has ever done such a thing before.' Wiremu stopped and looked at the proprietor, his eyes strangely intense, staring at something only he could see, or had just seen. His eyebrows

45

contracted downwards and lines appeared on his forehead, his mouth formed a tight line and his voice was slow and deliberate almost as though something, someone other than the affable Wiremu was speaking the lines through him. 'You see, it was not the priest that did this thing to Aporo. But his power makes him the *instrument*. What happened to Aporo was the ordination of some being, some place Mr. McRae, beyond this place, beyond our understanding.' The speaker paused for a moment. '*Aporo is in the clutch of a force impossible for us to understand.*'

Suddenly McRae was beginning to feel a little out of his depth. He understood about the quarrel, of course it definitely was *not* a good thing to strike a priest in Maoridom. By the look on the normally composed and serene countenance of Wiremu, he realised that the topic of Aporo's illness had ended and they talked of more pleasant things before Wiremu finished his drink.

As Wiremu walked through the village back to his whare, the sound of distant thunder from far off made him think of a thunderstorm and possible rain, but when he looked outside he saw it was a clear night and the stars were prominent.

Another rumble, this time the ground shook slightly then stopped.

He muttered to himself wondering what had caused that.

*

By the third week of Tuhoto's fatal pronouncement, the chief's condition was a lot worse. He lay in bed most days now. His wife, driven to distraction, was at a loss. What really hurt was that she had called a village doctor who promised he would come and do something but he seemed loath to keep his promise.

'Oh my dear Ngareta, your husband. 'Yes yes indeed, I shall be there tomorrow, indeed I shall. Yes, have no fear.'

Now it was three days later and the village doctor had not turned up. She simply couldn't understand why the man hadn't attended to Aporo. A month ago he would have come immmediately on being told the chief was unwell. Unknown to her the doctor, Atawai Letoro, had heard from one of the councillors present that night about the Tohunga's curse. 'I would dearly love to help out the headman, but what if I do? It would be absolute tapu to go against a kanga placed by Tuhoto! The curse, I was told was the fatal matae atua. In my own lifetime I have never known the curse to be applied, least of all to a Chief of the Ngati Hinemihi. The placing of such a curse by a great Tohunga is always fatal. I feel a great sorrow for poor Ngareta, a great sorrow, but I daren't go near the place, not now. If I try to make him well I am attempting to remove the curse placed by Tuhoto. I mean, who would go there, would you Ata?'

'The addressee's eyes bulged in fear and he simply shook his head as if to utter even a word would be most incautious.

*

It was Wiremu himself who turned up one morning, not for breakfast but to visit his friend.

Unlike many of the tribe he was not in absolute dread of the Tohunga. To continue his friendship with Aporo, to sympathise with his family, was not to violate a tapu neither was it, in his mind, incautious to do so. He knew Tuhoto and he regarded him as someone special but not necessarily malignant or spiteful. Of course the hara had been committed, the kanga applied, and he both understood and accepted the punishment. That was no reason to abandon Aporo and he would continue that friendship until, well until whatever was to come. Secretly he feared the worst. If only the chief had not lost his temper, despite being goaded into a reckless anger by the old man.

This morning the chief was not there.

'He's gone out to get some fresh air. Maybe that will increase his appetite, what do you think Wiremu?'

'Yes…So, how's he looking Ngareta?'

'Frankly terrible, he looks so weak and he's lost so *much* weight. What can I do? I feel…'

'Ngareta,' Wiremu interrupted. 'I must tell you something. Has your husband told you anything, anything at all?'

'No, I heard him one night, in his sleep. One word kept coming up. I thought it sounded like Tuhoto. He said it a number of times but the rest was too confusing and I couldn't understand his words. Perhaps he was thinking of asking the Tohunga for help.'

'No Ngareta, quite the opposite. Listen to what I have to say. I'm afraid that you're going to find my

48

story upsetting, very upsetting, and I must have your word that you do not mention it to your daughters.'

Wiremu told her the whole incident starting with the meeting one month previously, the tirade from the old Tohunga, and her husband's rash action that resulted in the application of the curse and subsequent break-up of the meeting.

Ngareta was too upset to speak for at least five minutes then she broke down, weeping silently to herself. Wiremu would never normally have dreamed of touching the wife of the Ngati Hinemihi's chieftain but he could not bear to see her sorrow and he placed both of his hands gently over the woman's shoulders.

It was like that when Te Wharekaniwha saw them, standing just outside his whare. He moved judiciously away. On the tribal chieftain's face was a look of great sadness and sympathy for his wife but also for his lifelong friend, whom he knew felt greatly for his wife's plight and her distress. Sooner or later, Wiremu would have felt it his duty to tell her what did happen that night, between himself and Tuhoto. He was glad because it had been too painful for him to recount the story, most of all to his family.

He turned round and walked towards the lake. The sand was soft to his feet and he was tired with the effort. He sat down and for the first time began to think rationally about the whole event. Yes, he'd been out of his mind with rage that day. Tuhoto was right, of course. His tribe had been misled, worst of all by himself, placing far too much value on things that were not important to his people. He had also desecrated the gods, displeasing them when he placed

49

the pakeha coins where previously the shell had been, removing that most valued and prized possession of the tribe, the life force of the paua.

He could see it now with absolute clarity. His argument with the Tohunga had been fruitless and caused his downfall. It had been his own greed and his pride that led to this state. Gold coins to replace the eyes of the gods. What a thing to do! You could not eat gold and he had worshipped gold more than his gods who had served his people ever since they set foot on TeAroha. *That* was the effect of the curse and it was not the priest who had deemed his fate but the gods of his people. Not the Tohunga!

Tuhoto had been the instrument, not the cause.

The revelation opened for Aporo Te Kaniwha, the portal of realisation, his life working its way in a series of gyres, and he saw in its entirety the absolute essence of his being. There was no voice in his head now, other than the decree of the timeless visitor, cloaked in the cobwebs of time, who had claimed him all of his life and had assailed him with words that flailed all doubt from his mind, revealing this moment of truth, and in its acceptance knowing that his spirit, not that of him which was corporeal, but his spirit, was–inviolate.

He realised that he would die, very soon, and now it did not matter and he had to tell Wiremu of what had been revealed. In his weakened state he found the strength to stagger back to his whare. His wife saw him and she saw in his eyes his moment of release. Wiremu had left a few moments before he entered his whare. His voice was frail but somehow it was as though the tension of the last three weeks had left him and she was relieved.

'Ngareta, send for Wiremu, has he eaten here today?'

'Today no, but he did come and...' Ngareta paused, for a moment her face an open book, then she added, 'he spoke to me.'

'I was away. He spoke to you, yes that is good.' He said nothing but looked directly at his wife. 'My dear, I could not bear to tell you myself, and he has done well, a true friend. Now, can you send for Wiremu please?'

'At once, yes.' She spoke to her daughter who sprinted down the slope of the whare and shouted to Wiremu that he should come back.

Aporo was sitting down when Wiremu entered, a change from seeing the chief lying down, in his weakened, helpless state. Ngareta left the room as he moved forward to sit next to his friend.

'Take some food with you when you leave, Wiremu.' The chief pointed to the table in the centre of the room. 'Ngareta has tried her best but you and I know the cause.'

This was the first time he had spoken to his friend about the curse placed upon him by Tuhoto, and he was saddened by the look of regret on Wiremu's face. 'Apart from that first night, you and I have not spoken of this thing. I have avoided speaking of it, hoping it would pass, but my end is written in the stars, as sure as day follows night,' he laughed, 'or is it, night follows day, I can never get it right.'

'Oh Aporo, my friend, I have been shocked by it and now it breaks my heart to see you like this. It has been…'

'No, no. It's…it's all right, your grief for me is that of a true friend. But there is something else, it came to me this morning, listen.'

The chief picked up a bowl of water and sipped it slowly. His hand shook as he put it down. 'This is about all I can take and in very small amounts, but it is enough to sustain my thoughts and that is all. The curse was absolute.'

'Yes.'

'This morning I understood fully.'

'Then you are resigned to your fate, Aporo. A Maori warrior, a noble, fears death not at all. But what land of dreams we go to, when our bones turn to dust. That is the fear. This we discussed before.'

'And that is what I have understood. Today I accepted fully, for the first time, what I had done and what I brought upon myself. But, there is something else Wiremu.'

'Yes?'

'Tuhoto. You see, it was not he who placed the curse. He was the divine instrument of the gods. Vengeance lies in their hands alone, and it is *they* who have punished me. Tuhoto, I forgave. As the Tohunga he simply performed what he was born to do. '

'But the after-life. Remember the matae atua that he placed upon your head covered that as well, all the horror of your soul wandering the land of dreams…'

'Which will not happen now!'

Wiremu understood the absolute certainty of his speech and the import of his friend's revelation. He believed now, implicitly, in what the chief was saying but he had to ask all the same. 'I believe this Aporo, but how did you know?'

'It was in my moment of acceptance. What followed was that in my heart I forgave the Tohunga and realised my great sin. At that moment, Wiremu, I saw the fantail dancing over my head. He came close, circling the skies dancing across my face and then I knew for certain.'

'What it is that we see when a truth has been manifest to us. The symbol of release.'

'I have been absolved, Wiremu. The matae atua will apply, but only up to the moment of my death. Beyond that now it cannot reach me.' He saw the look of relief on his friend's face and in his eyes.

'Well...thank the gods for that!'

'Truth, Wiremu. A wonderful thing, the gods see it and they know it. Acceptance lives in truth.'

'And truth in acceptance, so they are merciful.'

'Mercy? Perhaps. I was thinking of justice.'

The chief had become exhausted with his effort and Wiremu helped the man to his bed before he walked back to his dwelling. It came to him that it was fitting for a chief of the Ngati Hinemihi to understand fully the meaning of these things. The truth had been passed on to him now and he in turn would reveal this to the others at their next meeting.

*

Recently the mountain had been rumbling and once or twice Wiremu had felt the ground shake

53

beneath his feet. He had to go to Rotorua within the next three days. Sadly he wondered if Aporo would last up to then. When a person, be it man or woman, fully accepted their moment of release, their end followed soon after. Wiremu remembered also something else that was spoken by the Tohunga at a recent meeting with some of the elders.

This one happened very recently, at least a month after the slap. The Rangatira, Keepa Te-Rangipuawhe, had been present along with some of the elders belonging to the Ngati Hinemihi. It was Keepa himself who had told him what had happened. Apparently, Tuhoto Ariki had vilified the whole tribe for their debauchery, caused no doubt by the huge amounts of money that was flowing into the village and the subsequent excess of alcohol. Keepa knew about the previous meeting, a month ago, when Aporo had struck Tuhoto in front of the elders.

'Oh no! You're not going to tell me he's cursed another of our members.'

Keepa smiled then looked serious again. 'No, thank the gods. He might have come close to it when Matiu Iorangi said that he was talking nonsense. There was no curse but it certainly got the old man fired up.'

'Matiu is one for speaking out of turn, he's done it before. Well all I can say he was lucky. What did he say to Tuhoto?'

'He told him, straight out, that he was talking nonsense, but he apologized soon after.'

'As you say, thank the gods for that. Did the old man react?'

'He stormed out but it was what he said that concerned me as he left. I managed to catch a few words but frankly, it was enough. It was, *orange rain...destruction...*and his final words. *'...great mountain...it will speak...'*

'The mountain will speak. May Maui protect us! I don't even want to think about that.'

'When I returned to the village I saw two moreporks flying low over the water.'

'A bad show. Morepork in the forest is a good symbol. Morepork across the waters of Lake Tarawera, bad. Flying low, the worst possible omen.'

*

That night Wiremu dreamt that he was in the forest with his wife. She looked beautiful, about the same age as Ngareta, soon to be the widow of the former chief and his dying friend, Aporo.

His wife wore the beautiful cloak that her father had presented to her on their wedding day. A faint breeze blew a wisp of dark hair across her face and in the characteristic gesture he had loved to watch, she passed her hand across her forehead, pulling the strand away from her eyes to join the shining abundance that cascaded over her shoulders. Her feet moved lightly across the soft floor of the fern-covered forest and her dark eyes shone like two stars as they looked at him.

'What are you doing here?' he asked her.

'I came to see you Wiremu.'

'I...thought you'd be at home, I didn't realise you had left.' He was confused now so he added, 'It's nice that you're here anyway. Walking?'

55

'Yes, that's nice. We'll walk.' He felt doubt and worry nagging at his mind. What was it? He wanted her to stay with him and he asked her not to leave.

There was a look of inevitability about the way she was this morning and for some reason it filled him with dread. And her eyes were–sad.

'I can stay with you a short time but I will *have* to leave, you know that.'

He wanted her to stay and he couldn't understand why and then he knew. Knew that she had left him, a long time ago. 'It's been so long, but it's wonderful...you look so good,' he added. 'I go to Aporo's house for breakfast now.'

She laughed at that. 'I know.'

'But that will end soon. Aporo...'

'Yes, it will. When he comes I will guide him, he will be safe. The Kanga will no longer apply after his death. Now, there is something I must tell you Wiremu.' Her eyes searched his face. 'You must leave this place. Your destiny is no longer here.'

'Leave, but why, why here?'

'A storm is coming, a storm so terrible it will be the end of days here. The tribes need their leader and your destiny is to lead the tribe. You will be the Rangatira.'

He wished that she could stay, stay here, or that he could go with her, but she was fading as though her time in this world of substance was running out. She spoke again, her voice urgent. 'When we meet again we shall be together for all our time, but that is not for the present. Wiremu, your people need you ....leave now ...now ... now....'

He awoke suddenly and found he was crying like a child. There had been no doubt in her words that he must lead his people; that they would meet again, and his grief was replaced by a quiet resolve. Did she not say she was always with him? But not yet, not now. Her face was imprinted into the darkness of the whare, slowly fading, like in the dream and the room retreated back into its blackness, its silence. Yes, the dream was an omen and he *would* leave. The Tohunga's words, a prophesy or his own judgment placed irrevocably onto the tribe and he did not any longer doubt for an instant, either his words or his power.

NINE

Legend

The entity, perched on one side of the crater, surveyed the land below. Even though it had not been outside the depths for a thousand years, the creature knew this place well, a land that the tiny creatures existing upon its plains called, 'home.' Time mattered not at all, a second, a minute, a century, a thousand years. Unlike the humans that inhabited its territory, it felt no anger, no joy, no emotion other than its own dormant power and an ability to feel amusement in variety. The creature knew and understood the habits of humans. It was, by their years, measureless in age. Old before the ape-like hominids that grunted and jabbered, living in small caves below the mountains and in the dense forests. With its inherent ability to move across continents and seas, it had eventually come to see the first humans arrive in their small canoes, inhabiting the place that they named as Te Wairoa. The humans had a very short life span, they reproduced their own species and lived off the land. The creature laughed to itself and its laughter sounded like distant thunder and the humans would look up and fear what they thought was the mountain that had been its home for centuries.

For variety the creature had begun to manifest itself to the humans. It took the form of that which they called a, 'demon:' twenty feet high, its skin hard and leathery, the hands and feet sprouting talons. The huge tail swept back and forth scattering trees and lumps of earth. Folding its giant wings about itself, the creature resembled a small hill as the tribe passed back and forth in small groups looking for food, for flesh, for fruit and leaf. The creature unfolded its leathery wings and roared in fire and black smoke. The humans that were not burnt to ash stood transfixed in their fear then fled in terror. The demon's vast maw was a cavern, ringed with fire. It plucked a handful of the creatures, male and female, and swallowed, feeling their flesh, their salty substance as they burst and dissolved in the cavern that was its gut.

Often the entity would sit on the top of the mountain they had named, 'Tarawera,' and consider the absurdity of their existence. The humans themselves were a paradox, weak and helpless in their futile existence, yet there was something that had always puzzled the entity. It had begun to realise that one of their kind had a power to summon, to communicate with creatures other than its own species. The humans, creatures of habit, had names for everything and they had named this human, 'Tohunga.'

True to form, the Tohunga had identified the entity and named it, 'Tamaohoi.' At first the creature had laughed, amused by the antics of the Tohunga. It doubted whether the Tohunga was any more intelligent than its own species but it had let the Tohunga live, interested in his ability to tell the future, to heal his species.

One day during its raid on the humans, the creature had plucked this Tohunga from among the terrified inhabitants of the village. To its surprise the human was not afraid and for a moment Tamaohoi held the Tohunga over its cavernous mouth of fire, because in its tiny voice it was speaking to Tamaohoi, or perhaps to someone other than itself.

At that instant Tamaohoi dropped the Tohunga back to the earth as it felt a blow like the pressure of a giant hammer against its back and was flung to one side. Astonished, it turned and saw a vast form standing before it. The blow had been fierce and more powerful than the blast that came from the furnace below the mountain and it felt, for the first time in its existence over a thousand millennia, shock and a new emotion–fear. Simultaneously with the fear came rage in the knowledge that a human could have done this. It could see the giant clearly now, a humanoid, that resembled the tiny people below but vast in its dimensions and its scope.

Tamaohoi enlarged itself and struck out at the enemy with its tail. The humanoid increased its size immediately. Catching the tail, it swung Tamaohoi around and threw its bulk with immense force, away from the habitations of the tiny creatures, whose form his enemy had taken.

Dazed at the speed of this encounter, Tamaohoi landed with a crash against the earth at the top of the mountain. Surprised and hurt, it stood up, determined to fight the creature, to drive it from its domain, when it saw the humanoid standing above it. The creature had no emotion other than to look deeply into the face of Tamaohoi before it spoke.

'You have lived alone. Often I have watched you, tunnelling through the mountains, eating fire and drinking from the molten ponds below the surface. You would visit lands remote from here, flying across forest and lake. Your power was great but you transgressed the natural order when you chose to eat my people. Hear me now.

'I am Ngatoroirangi, the first of all Tohungas to enter this land, and the guardian of my people. Your days of spreading torment across the earth are gone. Let the earth and its inhabitants flourish. Now your home will be inside this mountain, never to come to the surface. Only a Tohunga of great power can release you from the deep. Your release, if at all, will be to perform a duty upon the order of the Tohunga. Go now! I have opened the door, and once opened I will close it. You are never to return.'

The giant humanoid lifted its hand up to the dark threatening sky, seized a jagged bolt of lightning, and in a burst of speed plunged it into the earth, creating a gaping hole in the side of the mountain called Tarawera. For thousands of years the mountain had been the creature's home but never, until now, its prison. It went into the darkness. The humanoid sealed the hole in the mountain with its massive foot, so that Tamaohoi would remain below ground until the earth itself had reached its end of days, or until the creature was summoned to come out of its prison.

The action of the creature that had condemned Tamaohoi to a subterranean existence had altered the consciousness of Tamaohoi and for the first time in its existence the creature that had hunted humans, understood and respected the Tohunga.

Banished, Tamaohoi spent its years plunging through the under-earth beneath the sea, through the dark caverns through endless rivers of superheated rock, speeding down into the mantle of the great mountains, boring through tunnels of earth but always coming back to the mountain named Tarawera that had been its prison.

*

This morning, after a thousand years, Tamaohoi had heard the call of the Tohunga and hurried to the mouth of the volcano. The entity noted the regiment of ancient warriors who had long left their role in human affairs but returned to the call of this man, the most powerful of all Tohungas. The giant's arrival created a quick burst of fire and smoke, small enough to go unnoticed by the people living in its shadow.

After being held prisoner within the mountain for a thousand years, it had been released. Tamaohoi knew the name of this Tohunga, the great Tuhoto Ariki of the tribe that lived in the village of Te Wairoa. The Tohunga's order had been specific and Tamaohoi understood clearly the terms of his release. The prophesy had been fulfilled by the authority of the Tohunga.

I, the Tohunga, give you sanction to do this thing. Your fire will purify the land.

A great Tohunga to do this, despite the long banishment imposed upon him by the invincible humanoid summoned centuries before by another priest of this same tribe. Released and empowered, Tamahoi had begun preparations deep within the mountain. Working along the fiery channels he had begun to assemble their awesome and destructive force, diverting each tributary into a series of four major cones fuelled by the churning millpond, now in the final stages of preparation. It was nothing for the giant to control the liquid fire, sometimes using its great hands then with its breath, charging the volcanic cones with enormous pressure that would soon become unbearable. He would hold back the mounting energy of molten fire until the Tohunga's call to inflict death and the absolute obliteration of this place.

The creature's laughter sounded through the depths of the mountain and its open maw exhaled gusts of black smoke and fire, heard below by the humans in thunder and a sudden shaking of the earth. For the first time in his existence Tamaohoi felt a happiness approaching ecstasy, knowing the suffering and death that he was about to inflict on the tribes.

Leaving the four cones of magma to gather their power, he sped to the central core of the earth and entered the cavern, the home that belonged to the dogs of destruction. Fire was absent from this place of eternal blackness, a distant cavern below the earth. Tamahoi picked up a boulder and struck the black, basaltic walls, setting up a prolonged resonance that echoed through the earth. At the same time it raised one hand above its head, causing flames to illuminate the cavern that had been in absolute blackness for thousands of years. The massive form stretched outwards and its claws raked the stone floor of its cave as though it were soft clay.

The creature's mouth opened and closed several times, then the yellow orbs for eyes noted the giant that had interrupted its slumber.

'You have chosen to awaken me. Either you have work for me or....'

'Work it is, and such work.' Noting the implied threat from the entity, clearly irritated by this abrupt disturbance of its sleep, Tamaohoi added, 'We have been summoned. By the Tohunga.'

The dogs were never easy to direct and always moody. If the call was for nothing they could attack whoever interrupted their thousand-year slumber. One dog, two or three even, was nothing for Tamahoi, but the pack of dogs that would arrive was something it did not want to contend with.

The dark beast, fully awakened by now, approached Tamaohoi. 'The Tohunga you say. What is it?'

'He called me three days ago, and he was attended by a tribe of dead warriors. I am to release the mountain's fire, at last.'

The dog opened its mouth exposing a fence of daggers for teeth, the creature's face as always a mask of sullen indifference to things of the earth. 'All right. My work and the work of my dogs, is to eat what is deemed to be eaten. In time, even you will be eaten by my legions as we devour all matter in this universe. So, for now only this land that is bordered by the great lakes, you say?'

'Indeed. The Tohunga spoke to me, this is what he said. "Release the dogs of destruction and let your mighty voice be heard across the earth and your fires reduce to ash the greed that has poisoned my land." You are to strike fear in their hearts and I will release my fire from the mouth of Tarawera to obliterate all things that lie beneath the mountain. This, the Tohunga tells me, will purify the land.'

'Then he is right. For this I will need my dogs. They will spread fear and pestilence among those who have transgressed. My presence is sufficient. If we are summoned so it will be.'

'How? Will you then devour the humans? Remember when I devoured them a thousand years before it was forbidden for me to do…'

'No. Understand this Tamaohoi. There are things other than flesh that we devour. The lakes, the beauty that is here, the water that flows across the pink and white basins. They will be devoured by my dogs and before that, a warning. I will manifest the spectres of dead warriors to show themselves to the humans who dwell on the land, but their heads will be the heads of my dogs of destruction.'

TEN

Ariki was relieved that he had gone early up the mountain. He had felt the stifling heat emitted from the darkness of the massive fissure. The mountain would speak for him, and its vast mouth would be the gateway for the storms of havoc. Of course he had no fear of the mountain or of its heat. He was safe from its lightning and from its malignant power that was about to be released. After that let come what may. This was the culmination of all his work.

He began to think practically so that when he arrived back in his village an hour later the first thing he did was to soak the soles of his feet in the cold water of the lake. Any thoughts of the warriors who attended his ceremony at the top of the mountain, were nothing to him. He had called them, they had arrived from the cosmic field, a membrane of existence separate from the earth and its orbiting planets, and yet as close as his elbow. They had served his purpose and that was all. Something that would have terrified those of his tribe or the unwanted pakeha, was simply a part of his sacrament. He was the Tohunga, his mind at one with the symmetry of the universe and its inhabitants. His feet cooled, he made his way back to the village, on the way picking a small bunch of yellow kowhai. For a moment he studied the plant. *Nothing lasts. When the mountain speaks you will be gone.* He took the sprig into his dwelling and placed it to one side of the room.

66

A woman, pleasant in her looks and disposition, somewhere in her thirties, entered the whare of the Tohunga when the sun had reached its zenith. Twelve o'clock by pakeha time. The hot dish of boiled and salted kumara was carefully placed in front of the Tohunga along with a pitcher of cold water. The old man would not drink any water other than that taken from the nearby stream. As always the service was performed in silence and in silence she would leave his dwelling. Especially today she knew there would be no dialogue between them as last night's tirade from the old man had been related to her by none other than Keepa the Rangatira of the district. Waiting for the old man to start his meal she recalled her conversation with Keepa, the consummate warrior, statesman and negotiator with the pakeha and the leaders of other tribes. He had seemed unusually worried, more so than the younger members at the meeting who had laughed at Ariki, not to his face but after he left, until Keepa had silenced them.

'…yes he was in a terrible fury. Cursed everyone, not just those who were at the meeting but the whole village, the outlying districts.'

'And did he speak to you afterwards? He usually does.'

'Nothing, his face was in a fury. I don't think I've ever seen Ariki in such a rage.'

'And I presume he included the pakeha.'

'They were blamed for everything. We were liable, according to him, for following in their footsteps.'

In the silence of the whare, Sophia, the guide, looked down at the priest who slowly drew the dish towards him and had a few sips of the water. She had turned and was about to leave, when to her surprise he spoke, his tone surprisingly calm, even polite.

'Te-Pea Hinerangi, as usual you bring me my dinner. I thank you.'

'No need priest, it is my duty. But thank you.'

She was standing in front of him when he asked her to sit down on a platform to his left. He saw the surprise on her face and chuckled to himself. 'So, Tepaea. How old are you now? Maybe thirty-something? You are a handsome woman Tepaea, handsome and kind. Of course you take the pakeha around our land but it is done in an act of kindness. Generosity and hospitality has always been the cornerstone of our tribe. '

'Well, yes sir. Thank you.'

'It is not your fault that they give large amounts of money to our people. That they have stayed, uninvited, to build their whares full of liquor. It is their money that defiles us. The money does nothing other than to make the men drunk and speak obscenities.'

The old man began to eat his food as he looked at her. She noted that the Tohunga never lowered his head to take each mouthful like most of the tribe but lifted the food up to his mouth, his head erect. 'They call you by another name. Sophia.' The fierce eyes for a moment lost their unaccustomed bonhomie as he stared into the wall of his whare. 'Of course, they cannot say our names correctly. That in itself is tapu. Nonetheless they will pay.'

She thought it best to agree with anything the Tohunga said, thus she got on well with him and gleaned information that was otherwise closed to the tribe. What he said next was a surprise.

'I have ordained that you will be safe Te-Pea Hinerangi. Go to your whare when the time comes.'

'Time? I'm not sure what you mean sir.'

'You will find out soon enough. The mountain has attended my curse and I have released the dogs of destruction. This is irreversible; it will come, and sooner than they think. Alright, go now. Be careful, note everything and prepare yourself for when Tarawera speaks.'

She went out into the bright light of day. Normally any affability from the old priest was a happy event for her and she suspected that he got lonely and liked her company. Today's conversation, in the light of what had happened last night, filled her with a sudden dread. ....*prepare yourself... when Tarawera speaks.* His rectitude, his good humour today, was what worried her. Ariki's normal surliness was perhaps more acceptable to her state of mind, especially after Keepa had spoken to her. So, what was it? More to the point, what had he done?

Unconsciously she inhaled deeply from the sprig of kowhai and tried to imagine a perfume, then moved it back and forth across her face, feeling the softness of the petals. An unaccustomed gift from the Tohunga, as she walked toward what was becoming the centre of the village, the impressive wooden tavern and its proprietor, Mr. McRae

These pakeha were a highly technical race, coarse in habit but clever in their skills. A warrior had no chance against their weapons, the powerful guns, and the terrible weapon they called a cannon. Nonetheless, Mr McRae was a civilized man, so indeed were the many tourists that had travelled to Te Wairoa.

When Tarawera speaks… What had Ariki meant? When he said that his face for a moment showed its habitual rage, the heavy eyebrows framing the fiery eyes forming sullen wrinkles around them and across his cheeks, his narrow mouth curving into a sneer. But when he looked at her it had gone and his smile was the sun appearing out of a storm cloud.

Te-Pea Hinerangi, newly christened, 'Sophia,' by the pakeha, looked troubled as she walked towards the tavern. Apparently Mr McRae had some people for her who wanted to have a look at Te Tarata and Otukapuarangi, called the pink and white terraces by the pakeha. Ariki was right. They could not pronounce the Maori language.

ELEVEN

Rapata

'So Rapata, there is something of urgency that you wish to tell me. Before I ask you what it is, why do I think it is something to do with my eldest daughter?'

The ferryman smiled wryly to himself and looked at the ground before replying.

'Sir, you are indeed right. I am leaving today for Rotorua, further if I can, maybe Tauranga.'

Hunapo studied the face of Rapata. A handsome man, the fine features of his tribe and its inherent honesty were inscribed in his face, ancestral lineage of the Te Arawa. He liked his direct approach.

I'm leaving for a distant place, I'm going now and ask your permission to take your daughter with me. That was his ancestors talking, respect and adventure. Yes, he had suspected right. But why was he leaving the village and why seemingly in such a hurry? The young man was well built from his years working the boats across the lake, firstly for his tribe, then later his earnings went up when he started taking tourists to see Te Tarara and Otukapuarangi. He had earned good money and instead of spending it on drink and shameful entertainment that had become symptomatic of the young men in his tribe, he had saved his earnings. At a time when there was so much

71

he could do he had decided to leave the village and take his daughter.

'You want to leave the village where both you and Kaheru were raised, can I ask why?'

The young man's face was an open book that said, you can ask but there are things that I cannot speak of. Long pause. A deep sigh heaved up from the young man and he said two words. 'Danger approaches.'

Hunapo's daughter sat at the back of the room next to her mother, looking anxious. The dark, luminous pools of her eyes intermittently flickered shyly down towards the earth, then, with a will of their own, rose to focus on the face of the ferryman standing before her father. She unconsciously flicked her long black tresses from across her face so that they flowed over her well-formed shoulders. Her slim figure gave the lie to the inherent strength of her tribe, bestowed with strong, well-shaped limbs and the full body of a nineteen-year-old. Like many women descended from the Te Arawa, her presence radiated a quiet dignity coupled to an innate resolve inherited from a tribe that wandered the oceans ceaselessly until their journey ended in this land, far removed from the continents of the world and shaped, on first sighting, as a white cloud of indeterminate length and, paradoxically, a land that received first the sun. She knew the young ferryman, trusted him, and whatever he said, she believed.

Ignoring the looks of longing that were passing silently between both the parties involved, Hunapo thought long and hard about what the young man had said before he spoke again.

'Have you worked this morning?'

'Yes.'

'Who was it?'

'Not a tourist sir, somebody local.'

'And who was that, Rapata?'

A long agonized pause. 'The Tohunga, Tuhoto Ariki.'

'I see. Obviously you do not wish anyone to know this.'

'Absolutely Sir.'

There was not much of village affairs that escaped his attention and he knew that the Tohunga used Rapata as his personal ferryman. 'Well, I will not ask you again. You have your reasons, and so does the Tohunga. To betray a secret or even the personal business of such a powerful man would incur a possible tapu. That being said, let me think before I give you my final answer.'

Events of the past few days, then of the month before went through his mind. He had heard of the terrible hara committed upon the person of the Tohunga. Tuhoto Ariki, of all people! The chief of the Hinemihi tribe had been on his sick bed for days, and from what he heard the man was so emaciated he was dying. He began to think about the extent of the curse, what had been said inside the meeting house, and then he knew for certain. He knew why Rapata could not speak and that the Tohunga had bound him to secrecy, the price for his safety, possibly his life. And now this young man was saving his own daughter to continue his line. Whatever the danger, his wife and their youngest daughter would stay here, and Maui protect them all. In that moment his decision was made. He turned to his wife, then his hand moved across his body and motioned towards Kaheru.

'Take her, my son. Take her and be safe. Go now and see Mr. McRae, he is a good man and he will provide for your journey. Tell him that I spoke to you. Your innocence and your strength have saved you, as it has saved Kaheru.'

Hunapo uttered the customary blessing of a father that gives his daughter to her future husband, after which Kaheru's mother gave them both enough food to take on their long journey.

*

'Hullo Rapata, not taking any customers today?'

'No sir. I have to go to Rotorua.'

The owner of the tavern pointed to a handful of newly-arrived pakeha, being helped out by the driver. 'Ten people today and we're expecting some more this afternoon.' He added, 'It could be a good day's work for you my boy, they will most certainly be visiting the terraces, you might pick up a pound or two, maybe more.'

Ah…yes of course sir. But I have to visit my grandmother, she lives in Rotorua.' He pointed to the coach. 'She's sick you see. I must go.'

'I see. Well in that case, of course. Good man, that's good to see, taking care of your grandmother before money. Good.'

'Sir, one thing.'

'What is that my boy?'

'I have spoken with Hunapo, and his daughter, Kaheru, wishes to travel with me. Her father and mother have entrusted her into my care.'

McRae considered the request. Only five people were going back to Rotorua in the coach today. There was nothing deceptive or dishonest about Rapata. He was one of the few local men left who would never drink liquor or even enter the tavern. 'Entrusted her,' meant that Rapata would probably marry the girl sometime in the near future.

'Well Rapata you're lucky. Yes indeed, there are in fact three spare seats, as most of the tourists are staying here another week or two. Alright my boy, off you go and tell Hunapo I said that's fine.

'Sir I thank you and how much…'

'You don't need to pay Rapata. After all, you and the lady will be taking care of the tourists. They're from Sweden and from England.' He winked at the young man hoping he would do well. 'Go on then, off you go.'

*

The small group of five pakeha consisted of three women, two of them with husbands. They were sheltering under the shade of a totara tree to one side of the rutted road. Rapata and Kaheru had secured their luggage at the rear of the carriage. This would be their first and only stop. Rapata had placed a small table in a shady area then carried the two cases, supplied by the tavern at Wairoa, that had been filled with food and drink for the journey. Kaheru had carefully laid out their meal very precisely on the table, then smiling at the tourists she decorated the

75

table with a bunch of wild flowers, which pleased them.

Not all of the tourists that came to their village were as kind as these. One of the men had suggested that they exchange a few of their sandwiches for some of the food provided by Kaheru's mother. This had been taken up by the others as a splendid idea and when they went back to Sweden they could tell their friends they had eaten the indigenous food of the Maoris and not that specially prepared for visitors from Europe.

After they had eaten, Kaheru was invited to sit with one of the ladies who talked to her and made a note of everything she said.

Rapata sat on the ground, some distance from the small group. The old man's warning was something he had taken seriously and with each turn of the wheel he was drawing further and further away from Te Wairoa. At that moment it came to him with a shock that his name in the old tongue meant, flame. The implications of that shocked him and he heard again the Tohunga's words after the events of this morning. The sighting of an apparition so terrifying, and beyond the ordinary events of anything on this earth: the unexpected manifestation of the great canoe and the spectral warriors that manned it. What had drawn him in were the dark pools of their eyes, the uncompromising gaze and the manifest intelligence upon the faces of the warriors. God! They saw him for what he was. That look said they knew him, his weaknesses, his strengths. Wherever they came from the entities knew him to the very core of his being and it turned his arms and legs to water. Yet the Tohunga had seen them as though the phantom warriors were there only for one purpose, to serve him, and he knew without a doubt now that it was the old Tohunga who had summoned them. A man whose power would awaken phantom warriors from their eternal sleep. The boat that he had steered all his life had become a living entity, gliding at impossible speed across the still, dawn water of the lake. Just once during the encounter he had heard a distant sound like the rumble of thunder and he knew it was the mountain. Apart from Ariki's order to stow his paddle, they had not spoken, and then Ariki had said those final words to him. *In three days from now you must be far from here... Do not come back. Ever.'*

The sudden realisation of what had really happened on top of Tarawera this morning came to him with a terrible finality and Rapata saw the end of days for Wairoa. A vision of flames, of forked lightning ripping through the sky, savage rumblings turning into massive blasts of thunder, rivers of liquid fire so that even the strongest of his tribe would be as minute grains of sand in the awesome maw of Tarawera's anger and vengeance. No, it was not the mountain. It was the priest who had caused this, an event not yet arrived but soon, very soon, to spread its pestilence across the land of his tribe. He, Tuhoto, had made Tarawera his instrument of vengeance. An *utu, placed upon his tribe's greed and its subsequent descent into the debauchery and shamefulness of men who had once been great warriors. He had been helped in this by the men he had seen in the waka taua. The great warriors of that historic and glorious past had been summoned to destroy the young men and women who had transgressed. The tragedy in this was that the innocent would suffer, along with the guilty. But then, in the mind of the Tohunga, they were all culpable.

One of the women looked in his direction, about to ask him to fetch some water. Seeing the young man's face she looked away for the moment. She would ask later, loath for the moment to disturb him.

*

They arrived in Rotorua that evening and Rapata, who had never left his village, was amazed at the sight of so many carriages, tourists and large buildings that dwarfed in size even the tavern of Mr Mc Rae. There was no need any more to dwell on his experience with the Tohunga. He had accepted his own role in the events but the fear that had possessed his spirit had gone, forever. What had happened on the lake was a pact between the Tohunga and himself.

The boxes and trunks belonging to the European visitors were taken off the wagon and in his broken English he asked them if they had liked their stay.

'Yes my dear fellow. Absolutely! How lucky you are. I suppose you will return home tomorrow.'

'… go to Rotorua, and if you can, further. Do not come back. Ever.'

Rapata smiled politely at the man as he followed Kaheru down the stairs of the hotel.'

One of the ladies had stayed outside looking at a shop window. They were about to leave when he turned and spoke to her.

'Madam, excuse me, will you be leaving Rotorua?'

The lady smiled and thanked him for taking up their luggage. 'Yes, tomorrow morning. We will catch the eight o'clock coach to Tauranga.'

His English was not up to explaining any portend of disaster and he spoke haltingly. 'That is good. Leave soon…before…before…there is much danger madam.'

It was obvious to her that he meant what he said. He had been a very sincere fellow, and he and the young Maori woman were very helpful. As he was about to leave she thought about his warning and asked him, 'What danger is that?'

'Madam…much…very bad.' He made a gesture using both hands in a sweeping motion upwards and that seemed to be all he was prepared to say. Great danger? Did he mean here, or in his village with the wonderful terraces? She felt a little sorry for him now and for the beautiful young woman. They had already turned to leave when she said. 'We're leaving in the morning, why don't you journey with us, to Tauranga? From what I hear, there's plenty to do for young people like yourselves, and you could help us on the journey. I did like so much talking to Kaheru.'

'Madam thank you.' He sounded doubtful.

'We'll need someone to act as a help along the way. Same as before.' She added. 'I know the others will be happy to see you.'

He had already told her that he was going back home but she understood. It was almost as if the Tohunga had spoken through this Swedish woman and he made up his mind. 'Yes, we will come.' He glanced across at Kaheru. 'Thank you madam.' Rapata left her walking down the road that led out of Rotorua and towards the town centre. They would stay with an uncle until the morning. He could always do something useful. As far away from Te Wairoa as possible.

'Do not come back. Ever.'

The lady's name was Inger Lindau and in the light of what was to come, she would remember the look on Rapata's face long after she returned to Sweden. Inger would talk about it to her friends and of the astonishing truth in a young man's warning.

TWELVE

A small group of visitors gathered outside the hotel run by Joe McRae. Clara Johnstone, living presently in Auckland, was a friend of Sophia from her previous visits to Te Wairoa. She introduced the guide to the five ladies and two gentlemen. 'Sophia is an absolute natural, you'll love her.'

What had been labelled recently as the eighth wonder of the world, the great pink and white terraces, waited for them. As ever, Sophia was only too happy to join in the conversation as the first introduction to boiling fumaroles and steam venting from parts of the lake could be a little daunting and she knew that it gave them confidence in the trip. In any case she liked them and enjoyed their company.

The tourists were from England with the exception of one woman, a well-built lady in her mid-thirties from Austria.

'Oh ya ya. I haf of this famous, how you say, the pink and white staircase, known.'

'Actually I think they are called terraces, Anita.' Helen Hunt had made friends with the stalwart Anita Schwartz from Austria, whose laughter at her own mistake set the others off.

'Oh ya you are right, excuse then please mine English.'

'Not at all dear, your English is perfect, isn't it Sophia?'

'Up to degree standard,' said the guide, adding, 'Anita is absolutely right, we are about to see a stairway, the stairway to heaven.'

'I can't wait to see that. Sophia,' Helen added, 'I've heard that if you pour whisky down the mouth of the vent at the top it lets off steam.'

'Waste of whisky' laughed the guide. 'Pour it down mine and I'll let off steam.'

They were approaching the stream that fed into the lake now and the conversation subsided as the guide halted abruptly and stared in shock at what she was seeing. She said nothing.

Clara Johnson had been down to the terraces many times, always with Sophia. 'Oh my stars! What's happened here? Where's the water?'

The guide studied the conglomerate of shell, pumice and dark clay left behind where the water had been–yesterday, the day before and a thousand years before that.

The new people were unperturbed. 'What do you mean, no water? Haven't we come to the lake yet?'

'There should be a stream somewhere, right here. It feeds into the lake.' Clara's answer sounded humorous and the tourists, thinking it was a practical joke, started to laugh. It was the look on Sophia's face that was of concern. Seemingly, the guide was staring at the dry bed of stone and earth, but her eyes were distant, and they were troubled. Her speech was slow, as though speaking to herself, and they did not understand now what she was saying. '... *note everything and prepare yourself when Tarawera speaks...'*

Clara knew that nothing ever perturbed the guide. She spoke softly so the others couldn't hear. 'What's that...what do you mean?'

The guide lifted her head and Clara realised that Sophia had been somewhere else.

'You said something about preparing yourself when Tarawera speaks. I think that's what you said, dear.'

'Oh. Did I really? My goodness Clara, I was day dreaming.'

But ...the water?'

'Oh! Nothing to worry about. This has happened before, tides you see. Tarawera always does something to surprise... what's that English saying? It keeps us on our toes.' The guide called out, her voice carrying across the banks, and they saw two boatmen running through dense bush that bordered one side of the lake. They arrived, panting from their swift run down the hill, followed by three Maori women who would travel to their habitation at one end of Lake Tarawera.

The crewmen were shocked at the lack of water and were about to say something when jets of steam vented through cracks in the earth, followed by a prolonged hiss and the sound of rushing water beneath the ground. The event had startled them enough to halt all potential for conversation, as though some inhabitant that existed below ground had breathed out. The subterranean visitor continued to make its presence felt. A sudden gurgling, the sounds of moaning, then as if by some remarkable alchemy, some trick or sleight of hand from the subterranean magician, water flowed rapidly back into the stream. The boat that had floundered on bare earth where there had always been water, floated conveniently up towards them, once again offering its services, bobbing up and down at the unprecedented actions of the water.

Sophia spoke in Maori to the boatmen and Clara Johnson noted that they looked worried. Whatever she had said was not for the tourists. As yet the rest of the party were untroubled, assuming this was the normal course of events.

'Right people, this is all for our entertainment. It's a case of, now you see me now you don't.' The guide was her usual self and all was as it should be as they got back into the boat. The unusual rise and fall in the water today caused the vessel to bob up and down. The men were about to row when the boat went down rapidly and once again, they were on dry land.

As yet nothing had been said, no explanation offered to the tourists as to why this was happening and Clara guessed it was because it had never happened before. She suspected also that Sophia's jest was to ease the trepidation of the newly arrived tourists. There began a discussion in Maori, the shrill voices of the three local women added to the discussion then all conversation ceased when the unexpected event happened again.

The lake's clamour was a deep, amplified ululation of grunts, hisses, whistles and groans, as though the entity that lived below the earth had decided to add its own voice as a prelude to their journey across the lake. It momentarily masked all conversation with a succession of rapid sounds coming from underground, accompanied by the lost water that for the second time rushed into the creek. This part of the lake, which had become barren, now filled rapidly with water that gushed up from below the ground.

Whooo… ssshhhh… shhhhhh aaahhhh… hooooo… whhhhooooo…Aaahhhhh…

They listened in silence, the faces of the tourists a mixture of awe, and by now some unease, with the exception of Sophia and the priest, Father Kelleher, who remained calm as the lake began to fill and then rise several feet above the normal height.

The Maori boatmen looked openly worried and for the first time the tourists appeared concerned. Their anxiety increased as they heard the hurried conversation between Sophia and the boatmen, which continued for about two minutes before the guide's explanation in English to her charges.

'Well ladies and gentlemen, and you Father Kelleher, I see this event now as being highly unusual. To those of our party this morning who have not been here before, I have asked the advice of our boatmen and they have agreed that they want to continue.' The guide looked, as always, composed and smiling. 'I'm sure now that all will be fine. The lake's there, the terraces wait for us, so if you are ready we can settle down now and leave.'

Sophia did not say that she had been so concerned that she had suggested calling the trip off altogether but the men, despite their fear, had accepted reluctantly that it was just some temporary fluctuation and all would be well. It was a fine day and they were not happy about losing the five pounds in revenue from each overseas passenger. The three Maori women were the only ones still looking very worried. Sophia spoke sharply to them and they stopped talking altogether, trying unsuccessfully to settle down in the boat.

They rowed out easily, riding on water that was considerably higher than normal. The experienced Clara Johnstone noted that weeds normally covering the surface were below the water. 'Sophia, look at the level of the lake. It's higher than I've seen it before.'

Sophia decided it was time for her to discontinue any pretence that what was happening was normal. 'Yes, you are right dear.' But then she added, with a note of humour. 'You must admit it is far easier to paddle.'

She spoke in Maori to the boatmen, and was pleased to see that after the initial shock they looked relaxed and confident as the journey continued towards the shimmering beauty of Te Tarata and the splendid pinks of Otukapuarangi.

They alighted on the soft pristine sands and had their tea and sandwiches while the boatmen rested to one side. Sophia encouraged her group to bathe in the lower pools of water and they were joined by the Maori women. The events of the morning were discussed openly and at times with light-hearted humour by the tourists. It was almost as though they were delighted to be the first people who had experienced the unusual event with the stream leading into the lake and would relate every detail of this experience to people back in England and in Austria.

Time came to leave and like many visitors before them the small group took a last look at the terrace. Steam floated lazily across the hot pools, on this clear day a deep reflected blue contrasting against the pink walls of sinter that folded uniformly down towards the lake. Sophia was about to speak to the boatmen, then she looked again at the terraces and it was as though she was seeing them for the first time. She did not want to go, not just yet.

'Time? I'm not sure what you mean sir.

You will find out soon enough. Alright go now, be careful, note everything and prepare yourself for when Tarawera speaks.'

*

The Maori ladies were due to be dropped off in a small habitation at one end of the lake as the canoe arrowed its way towards the next landing. To the tourists everything was a wonder. The temperature of the water seemed to fluctuate from cold to warm to hot. At one point the boatmen spoke to Sophia, pointing to a large area of steam venting across the surface. The guide, familiar with every part of the lake, spoke again in Maori and their rowers moved away from the dense warmth of the steam issuing from below ground. It seemed now that once again the Maori were looking concerned and Father Kelleher asked Sophia if it was usual to see steam on the lake surface. He noted that the guide tried to sound casual saying the lake had many moods and this was one of them. Father Kelleher smiled and said nothing more.

Mount Tarawera loomed in the distance as the boat skimmed through its reflection. Sophia was relating the story of the demon god that was part of Maori mythology, and according to tribal legend lived within the depths of the mountain, when one of the boatmen pointed to something moving across the water about a hundred metres ahead of them and to their left, coming near enough to pass across their bows. The boatmen looked surprised and spoke to the guide.

'What is it Sophia? The men look a little worried.'

'Well, it's unusual to see a craft of this type. It looks to me, and to my oarsmen, like an ancient vessel. We call it a 'waka taua,' or a Maori war canoe. We don't have anything of its kind here.'

As she spoke a mist formed, changing rapidly into a dense fog that seemed to blanket the approaching vessel. They could hear the chant of men as yet unseen: a doleful cadence of voices that, like their canoe, did not really belong here, and seemingly in time with the splash of the oars as they pushed into the water.

The cloud grew thicker, masking the unexpected visitors to the lake. All they could hear was the slow, deep intonement of the oarsmen, coming nearer to their boat. The sound resonated across the lake, deceptive in its origin, coming first from the boat, then at times surrounding them.

The cutwater shape of a prow sliced through the leaden fog, followed by the long aerodynamic shape, not meant for this or any other lake. Sophia and her oarsmen knew it as a vessel that carried their people across the seas, plunging across oceans, seasoned in all storms, lashed by wind and driving rain and powered by the bone, the sinew, the muscle of a warrior race that had won this land. Such was this craft, the womb and provenance of its people. What was it doing out of its time and why here with its grisly crew?

There were thirteen men in the war canoe, men, or what had once been such. Their faces were cadaverous, the bodies skeletal, eyes burning as they stared directly at the visitors, seeing them and through them as to some thing, some event that had been, or was to come. The leader inside the craft was standing upright and behind his crew, holding a spear which was pointing directly at Tarawera mountain. The faces of the spectral warriors appeared, gradually, to metamorphose into the heads of giant dogs. The canoe slowed down, passing in front of them and they heard, not the speech of men, but the prolonged incantation of the spectres inside the vessel.

The tourists, normally practical down to earth people, were confronted by a metaphysical event that was impossible to grasp or to interpret. The deep-throated dirge of the creatures and the close proximity to their own vessel had induced a trance-like shock that brought about a convolution of their senses, making fools of their present mortality. Time and substance had become illusory, the senses fragmented and unable to grasp or separate matter from illusion. The Maori crew, like the boatman Rapata, had lost all volition to row their passengers. Their legs and arms had turned to water.

Their visitors had come from the logic, the sweet-reason of companionability, of indescribable beauty, into the territory of a nightmare that was unforeseen, unwanted, and absolutely beyond their understanding, beyond their ability to cope with what they were seeing. They were in a land far removed from their own, taking part in the celebrations and the rites of her indigenous people, expectant of its inherent beauty. A country so remote that it received first the sun, things of the earth, pleasing and intelligible to the senses. The departure of the water this morning followed by its abrupt reappearance, were of themselves physical events of terrestrial forces that had substance, palpability, but the appearance of uninvited messengers from the field of the undead defied any rational explanation, and the group of tourists from Europe were out of their depth.

'In god's name...Sophia! What is it? Who... what are they?' The voice of Helen Hunt, hoarse, emerging weakly through the miasma, restored a weak attempt at a semblance of reason.

The guide was not prepared to calm their fears with false logic. She was the only occupant of the boat who stood firm, erect of carriage, and she answered as truthfully as she could. 'In god's name dear, they are the bones of warriors long gone from the earth. I'm sorry I cannot tell you more. This is the first time that myself, or anybody in Te Wairoa has seen this.'

Cool logic confronted the field of unreason and seemed, if that was at all possible, to calm them. Sophia, Te-Pea Hinerangi, stared at the sight, unable or unwilling to answer anymore as the waka taua with its pale ghosts passed by, apparently making for the shore, but never really getting there. Then she remembered Ariki's words or fragments of what he had said to her yesterday after he had allegedly been to the top of Tarawera.

'The mountain has attended my curse. I have released the dogs of destruction. This is irreversible, it will come and sooner than they think.'

The long aerodynamic shape made its way almost to the opposite bank and then before reaching the shore, the boat and the men inside appeared to melt into the ether and were gone.

*

By evening the village was alive with gossip and rumour. People in the village had seen the phantoms but not as clearly or in such close proximity as the tourists and their concern changed to a state of panic when the spectral faces had transformed into the heads of dogs.

Keepa had just come from an emergency meeting of all the elders to discuss the implications of what they had seen, when he met the guide going to the store for provisions. For this particular conversation, they spoke in Maori.

'Is it true Sophia that you were on the water at the time? From what I hear the boat stopped and approached your vessel.' He noted that the guide hadn't lost her sense of humour.

'Well as far as journeys to Otukapuarangi and Te Tarata go, this morning's expedition wouldn't rate as–special! Yes it was near, too near, and of course the tourists, who do not believe in these things, have no explanation.' Sophia described in detail what she and the others had seen. She was loath at first to tell him of the Tohunga's warning yesterday.

Keepa continued. 'At the meeting we have concluded this is a portent of bad things to come. What is your opinion? I know that you go to give the old priest his lunch every day. Did he say anything to you?'

'I'm afraid so. He said something about preparing myself for when Tarawera speaks. "The mountain has attended my curse." Something else, about releasing the dogs of destruction.'

The Rangatira looked worried. 'Then it appears you are right. I believe some people saw the faces of the warriors, the men or whatever they were, change into the heads of giant dogs. Was it as they said?'

'At first they had the faces of ancient warriors, no doubt about that. They looked like men who have been dead a long time. Then their bodies changed again, strong muscular bodies but, yes, with the heads of dogs.'

There was no questioning the logic of her account. 'Alright. I thank you for this. You may be interested to know that Rapata, the boatman who would ferry dignitaries across the lake, has left the village altogether. Remember he was the one who two days previously took Tuhoto Ariki across the water, allegedly to Mount Tarawera. I now believe the one hundred-year-old man *did* reach the mountain. How, no one knows, but he has much power at his disposal and he hates what we have become. Whatever happened on the lake that day caused Rapata to leave, taking Hunapo's daughter with him.

'I see his point of view Keepa Te Rangiwhuaphe. We were a diligent people who lived here. Descendants of the Te Arawa. We worked the land, fought our battles, honoured our women and children and perpetrated utu upon those enemies who betrayed us.'

The Rangatira's face showed unease, coupled with a sensitivity for all of his tribe. Personally he was not at all happy with the reckless amounts of money flowing into the village. Money was making them indolent and selfish, drunken, broken-down caricatures of all that a warrior should be. He had admonished a young man demanding ten pounds from a German woman, an artist who wanted to paint the pink terrace. In this particular instance the price had been lowered to one pound.

'We need the money for the tribe sir. Before this we were poor.'

'We were never poor.' Keepa became angry and shouted at the youth who at least had the grace to look ashamed in front of the Rangatira. 'You've had your money, now go, and stop pestering this woman. Run off to the tavern. We both know where this money will go.'

He thought again of Tuhoto's tirade at the council when the priest had pointed out the wealth that surrounded them, the wealth bestowed upon their tribe by Maui as a reward for their valour and their perseverance in finding this land after their years of wandering across the oceans to arrive home. There were many like the young man he had admonished, who had forgotten the gift from the gods and had begun to worship round bits of metal. As Rangatira he had planned to do something about this, like perhaps banning them altogether from the ale house, and he knew he could put his law into effect if he was forced into that position.

One of the chief perpetrators was Aporo Te Kaniwha, the chief of Ngati Hinemihi. The incident that had taken place in the meeting house one month previously had been reported to him by the elders. A disgraceful event when Aporo Te Wharekaniwha had actually slapped a Tohunga in front of the tribal statesmen. Slapping a Tohunga was one thing, slapping the man who had the dreaded power of Makutu, capable of applying a curse upon an individual, was another thing altogether. What on earth had possessed Aporo? Yes, greed, coupled to Aporo's inability to control himself. He knew absolutely how it would have happened. Ariki outraged by the sacrilege committed by those who had replaced the all-seeing eyes of the gods with pakeha money. Aporo Te Wharekaniwha was unable to see that at the time and so he could not possibly agree with the Tohunga, who of course was right. The chief had become greedy, seeing himself richer even than the pakehas, and the argument had started with neither man prepared to give in.

94

He turned his attention to Sophia again. It had been a little over three weeks since the slap and he asked the question out of curiosity. 'How is Aporo by the way? Have you seen him, heard anything?'

The face of the guide had a look of inevitability and concern. 'Seen, no but I spoke to his wife and daughter.'

'And?'

She shook her head, the eyes slanting towards the village then back to him. 'Apparently he has been ill for the last three weeks, possibly longer. He doesn't want to see anyone for the moment.'

'Have you seen him?'

'No. But I spoke also to his second in command, Wiremu. As you probably know they are very friendly.'

'Yes.'

'He's sick, very sick. Between you and me Wiremu told me that there is no question as to whether he will die or not, it is simply a matter of when. He talked recently to Aporo who is resigned to his fate.'

Keepa looked at the delicate-featured woman, the almond-shaped eyes, the calm assurance of her speech and her ability to put people at their ease. He noted how as always her actions were graced with an inherent dignity and the bearing of a high-born lady. No wonder she was well liked by both pakeha and by the tribe and what was more, trusted. The guide was a fine role model for any woman. His own daughter Herena had the same bearing, the same confidence, and he was glad he had sent her to study at a convent in Tauranga. Recently Herena had met an Englishman, a fine man of high standing in his own country, something that pleased him. He spoke to the guide again. 'Thank you for your information. As always my dear Te-Paea you can be trusted for your diligence, both in your work and your relationship between ourselves and the pakeha. I should make you an ambassador and send you out to meet important leaders from England.'

'The role of humble guide suits me just as well, sir.'

Yes, humility is a great gift, he thought, and you have it lady. He laughed softly to himself after thanking her for the information about Keepa and wished her well before the guide walked back to her well-built and sturdy whare.

Keepa thought again of the fact that Rapata the ferryman had slipped away, gone out of the village, and that after taking Tuhoto to the mountain. What had actually taken place there? Rapata had not spoken to anyone after that. Why had he left? Perhaps it was the old man himself who had told him to leave and he knew that his guess was correct. There were a lot of things on his mind and once again he thought of the worst insult that could possibly happen to a member of his tribe; slapping a Tohunga. Tribal utu was a deadly and serious matter, usually it involved reprisals of tribal conflict or personal revenge. In the case of a man with cosmic powers, what form would his revenge take?

An apparition upon the great lake. No, an *appearance* on the lake because what they saw was tangible, real, but coming from somewhere beyond the familiar, far removed from the rational world known to people.

The absolute chief of the time-honoured tribe of Ngati Hinemihi, reduced by words to his death. And a powerful Tohunga promising disaster upon his people, whose excesses had insulted the gods. In his mind he went back over Sophia's matter-of-fact recitation of events. Of course he believed it. What fatal snare of air then, had trapped these warriors of the undead, unable to escape? Or perhaps they had existed in that cosmic field, waiting for the summons of a powerful Tohunga that reverberated across the dimensionless desert of eternity. There was no doubt in his mind now and he knew with absolute certainty that it was the Tohunga who had awakened them to attend his sacrament. God! His head was reeling. With a terrible smile the Rangatira turned and walked away.

THIRTEEN

McRae had just placed a row of liquor bottles along a shelf behind the bar when they began to rattle against each other. Aided by his assistant, he removed the bottles and placed them inside a cupboard on the ground. The ground shook for about a minute then stopped and McRae walked over to reassure the guests.

'We have these occasional rumbles and shakes sometimes,' he explained, pointing in the direction of Tarawera. 'The old man up there complains a bit but we're used to it by now.'

They looked relieved. There was another tremor, lasting for a few seconds, this time accompanied by a sound of distant thunder. It was as the proprietor said and they laughed nervously, uncertain about McRae's apparent confidence. Then the shaking stopped altogether. A small cloud of black smoke issued from the mountain and was seen by one or two people sitting on the balcony outside. The shakes and the rumbling had been more frequent recently and sometimes McRae felt a slight unease.

He had spoken earlier to the Rangatira, Keepa Te Rangipuawhe, a man he admired for his common-sense and his sensitivity to any problems that arose between the indigenous peoples and the tourists.

'Well, Keepa I don't know. Have you experienced the tremors and the smoke coming out of the mountain before? I mean as often as this?'

Keepa had been here since his birth, in the scale of things far longer than the tenure of his friend.

'Well yes, but not to this extent. There have been instances in the past, say about twenty years ago, when the mountain was issuing black smoke and we had about one tremor a month but this is unusual.'

'I agree, then there's that bit about the phantom canoe last week. Whatever happened out there, it certainly had everyone talking.'

'Mm! You see the thing with my people is that...' The chief scratched his chin, uncertain about his next utterance and whether the tavern owner would place him in the category of another superstitious native. He knew however that McRae saw him as a man with balanced views on everything. He continued. 'You know of course that the chief of the Ngati Hinemihi tribe has died suddenly.'

'No! You're talking of Aporo aren't you? Well of course I do know him. This is a shock, how did it happen?'

Keepa grinned wryly to himself and looked at the tavern owner. 'Alright, I'll tell you. About a month ago, Aporo got into a verbal battle with Tuhoto Ariki...'

'Yes, the Tohunga, isn't that right? I've seen him now and again, from a distance you might say.'

'Alright, well the end of it was that Aporo, in a fit of temper, struck the old man across the face.'

McRae knew enough about Maori culture to look genuinely surprised. 'That's really very bad, a Tohunga?'

'It was in a public meeting, in front of the room full of tribal elders.'

'Really?' McRae looked down at the ground, shaking his head.

'He put a curse on Aporo, then and there. There was no song and dance, no shouting or abuse on Tuhoto's part. From what I was told he administered the curse quite calmly, matter of factly you might say, and placed what we call a matae atua, on the person of Aporo Te Wharekaniwha.'

'What's that?'

'The worst form of curse. It means the person under a curse like that will fall ill and die shortly.'

'Goodness. And do you believe that?'

'You probably know what I believe, the point is do you?'

There was a long pause between them before the tavern owner replied. 'Well the man has died. He was as far as I know hale and hearty, then he's gone. I'll tell you now Keepa, in answer to your question, yes I do believe.'

'Alright, now the bad bit.'

'Oh no, it's a case of the bad news, followed by the bad news. Now what's coming?'

Keepa smiled in amusement at McRae's choice of phrase then became serious again. 'I was at a meeting a few days ago, it was a month after the slap by the way. Again the old man left in a fury but it was what he said when the meeting ended, if you can call it that. They couldn't get out fast enough, let alone stay for the usual ceremony. Tuhoto was more or less talking to himself as he walked out in a temper. It was something about, the mountain will speak and we'll find out soon enough.'

'What brought that on?'

'He was in a rage about the antics of the young men and some of the older ones. Getting drunk, greedy, getting as much as they could out of your people and so on. Of course, your place came under fire, not you personally but the existence of the tavern. Anyway one of the elders at the meeting accused him of talking nonsense.'

'Ill-advised in the light of what's happened to poor Aporo.'

'Yes, well he never cursed anyone at that meeting. The fellow apologised to the Tohunga and that was that, but I saw his face and I did hear the comment about the mountain speaking. It scared me and, frankly, with these shakes and the mountain's recent activity, well, I don't know.'

McRae looked thoughtful before he spoke again. 'Superstition and belief? Let me tell you that pakeha can be very superstitious, Keepa, not just your people. Do I believe that certain humans, those like your Tohunga, can influence events of the earth? Yes I do and it worries me. English, British, European tradition as a whole is full of stories, some of them too near to reality to disbelieve that there *are* humans with the power to influence natural events on this earth. Well, we'll leave it there. I asked you and you've told me. Come have a small shandy, at least. You know, half lemonade half beer. Perhaps these tremors and the smoke will die down ....perhaps it will be alright.'

The chief was up to it and they retired to a separate table in the large tavern, slowly sipping the ale and for now, alone with their thoughts.

They were about to part later when the chief spoke again. 'Oh I almost forgot. That very next morning Tuhoto left the village. I know because I went to see him and two young fellows said he had left to go across the lake. When I asked why they said he told them he was going up the mountain. He was quite open about that, but of course he wouldn't say why.'

'But the mountain's impossible for him to climb, that can't be true.'

'Listen, the ferryman who took him across the lake was a young man called Rapata. He wouldn't say anything and a few people who saw him after that said he looked strange, shaken. Something happened when he took the Tohunga over the lake that he did not want to talk about. I've been meaning to have a word with him, but he's disappeared.

'Well, I can tell you now Keepa, you won't see him again and I'm certain of that.'

'How do you know?'

'He came to see me recently, and he seemed in a real hurry to go to Rotorua. He took a young lady with him as well. I can't remember her name.'

'Did he say where he was going?'

'No. But the way he spoke he seemed desperate to leave. I got him a trip on one of the coaches, along with his young lady.'

After McRae's information the Rangatira looked really worried. So too was the tavern owner.

'Alright. In that case something happened during the time that Rapata was with the Tohunga and whatever the event was, it made the young man want to leave in a hurry. *That very day.* Was it possible that Tuhoto told him something? Putting two and two together...what was it he said to Rapata that made him leave so suddenly?'

FOURTEEN

Today the pink and white terraces had never looked more spectacular. For those who had travelled across hazardous seas, there never was a day where they did not look better than the day before.

The rumblings coming from Mount Tarawera had become more frequent, yet a stillness prevailed and with it a sense of relief that the mountain had settled down at last. All was well and the great jewel in the crown of Aotearoa glistened and sparkled in the sun.

Deep inside the earth molten rock was being pumped upward by a vast entity, pushing with giant hands. The wind from its breath had the force of a thousand storms, to charge the lava with a dynamic force, far greater than at any other time. To one side the hound snarled, impatient to release his dogs of destruction.

'Soon, very soon now but not yet. My time for vengeance has arrived. Death, like a thief in the night, will come upon them.'

*

Morning turned to afternoon, a hot lazy day. The tourists bathed in the ponds, and explored Lake Tarawera. The usual performances from the indigenes brought enthusiastic cheers of appreciation and much applause from the tourists. They drank, talked and sang, took part in the evening entertainment, got drunk, had supper and retired for the night. The performers were happy as they went home counting their wealth knowing that tomorrow and tomorrow and the day after that there would still be money flowing as freely as the abundance that flowed from the great geysers over Te Tarata and Otukapuarangi.

*

McRae had assumed a counterfeit cheer for his tourists but he had been troubled, firstly by the recurrence of shocks and then his conversation with Keepa.

Keepa Te Rangipuawhe was in his own dwelling but he came out again and studied the mountain. He had felt a slight tremor or vibration of the earth below his feet that had persisted, strangely unlike the sharp intermittent jolts that had made him and McRae uneasy at the time. A full moon hung over the sky and in the cool night his breath sent out frosty air like the smoke from a cigar. He was about to go back inside when he caught a glimpse of the Tohunga walking past the meeting house, towards a small grassy knoll .

The Tohunga was focusing his whole attention on the village below, his mouth forming words, inaudible from where he was. Finally, he appeared to end his speech and with a calm deliberation the gaunt figure turned and lifted both hands in the direction of the mountain.

A silence had settled across the night, and he could no longer feel the vibrations that had persisted for the last two hours. The silence was uneasy, disquieting, and then he knew what it was. It shocked him. The flow of waters that had fed the great terraces had stopped, their tenure of a thousand years–ended. For a moment there was nothing at all.

'Do I believe that certain humans, those like your Tohunga, can influence events of the earth? Yes I do and it worries me.'

The pale lunar glow over Te Wairoa and the cool serenity of a clear night was obliterated from the sky as a blinding flash of lightning was followed by an immense detonation. Flames issued from the mouth of the volcano. The incandescence from the mountain's fire illuminated the Tohunga's face. There was a calm there that Keepa had not seen before, as Ariki's tributaries of retribution began a slow descent over the giant slopes of Tarawera.

Dark fiery clouds gathered overhead and he felt instinctively that he was seeing the end of days for Te Wairoa. As Rangatira, there was no choice for him other than the execution of his duty and he knew he would have to search for those caught out in the approaching storm, those too weak to help themselves.

People ran towards the meeting house because it was well built and they felt it might protect them. They came upon the tall, gaunt figure of the Tohunga. The priest had not followed the panic-driven flight towards the dubious safety of the shelter, he remained in the open upon the small knoll, hands back inside the folds of his cloak. Despite the urgency of their flight to safety, they stopped, as though under some compulsion to face, to hear, the man who was their Tohunga.

The priest's eyes reflected the fire of the mountain and in the orange glow of the sky, the moko writhed across his face as though alive as his words struck terror into their hearts.

'Look all of you here. Yes, you will die, I will die, the village will die and the beauty of Te Tarata and of Otukapuarangi will shatter into fragments and descend deep into the water and will be seen no more. That which they came here to see, that which corrupted our people, is forever gone. The angel of death is here and with the dark angel, the dogs of destruction will follow.'

Under the spell of his words, their eyes reddened by flame, his reluctant audience followed the priest's hand. A gigantic dark cloud of destruction that obliterated the stars hovered over the land, in its wake the orange river flowed from the jaws of the mountain, across the forests that had for centuries graced its slopes. Waves of molten fire swept across the great pink and white terraces, their indescribable beauty swallowed into the boiling morass beneath the lake.

The Tohunga raised both hands against the flames issuing from the maw of Tarawera as though he was in the act of warming himself in this cold night of the full moon.

'Ahhh...fire! Who can explain its immutable fascination, its cleansing flame, turning all matter back to its seed life, back to the elements from whence it came.' He spoke as though to himself, again in words so ancient that no one could decipher or understand. The Rangatira, Keepa Te-Rangi-puawhe caught a few words and they were enough to shock him even though it was not in his nature to feel the sudden jolt of fear. Ariki was chanting something in a language that no one understood, each syllable prolonged, a summons to someone or something, a sullen incantation against the deep rumbling of Tarawera, as he pointed at the fiery monolith, then slowly lowered his hands. For that moment, perhaps for the last time, the Tohunga turned and stared into the face of Keepa.

Silence, as though the mountain itself had drawn breath and ceased its rumbling.

A gigantic detonation of sound, sharp bolts of lightning sweeping across the sky, and then a furious column of fire erupted from the mountain. A blinding cone of white heat climbed impossibly into the sky, seemingly to pierce the fabric of the stars. The Priest's hand clawed across the sky, accompanied by his shrill cadence of death. A second white-hot cone burst out of the mountain, followed instantly by a third and then a fourth.

The initial detonation of four separate columns of fire was the prelude to a continuous roar of sound, attended by a giant storm of hot wind, generated by the flux of atmosphere above the mountain. It besieged the mind, making it impossible to think. They stood in silent awe, pakeha and Maori together, stunned by its lethal beauty. The smell of scorched earth and black smoke reached the village and stung their nostrils, lodging in their throats, but by this time they had fled into the night, into the dubious safety of their own frail dwellings. Tiny, inconsequential figures, illuminated by the fires of hell spouting from the earth and flowing down Tarawera.

Lowering his hands the priest of The Te Arawa turned away, his face impassive, the final ritual performed. They did not see or care to see the tall, wiry figure of the Tohunga turn and walk back towards his small whare and disappear into its darkness.

*

Joe McRae had done more than could be expected from anyone in the chaos and panic. Struck many times by fragments of hot earth and flying debris of scorched branches, he had struggled in the dark lifting people out of their helpless panic. Exhausted and unable to do more, he led them towards his shelter that was rapidly being covered in hot ash and lumps of scoria. Those he had rescued were crouched down on the hot earth, buffeted back and forth as the ground shook. They spoke not at all, consumed into the absolute blackness of the room.

For some reason, McRae had elected to stand, leaning against one of the solid, wooden walls, feeling the wood hot to his touch. A strange lethargy came over him and he thought that perhaps he was he was dying, maybe he was already dead and the mind was flickering with imperfect images of things that made no sense: people, places, disjointed events. The notion of his true state in the universe came to him, that he and those around him hoping to live were specks of cosmic dust that came and went and for the first time in his life, the shattered shell that was Joseph McRae understood the truth of his own mortality.

There were sixty people in Sophia's whare. She knew that of all the dwellings her whare had the best chance as the roof had been constructed from solid interlocking beams of rimu. The thatching would blow away in the storm of hot wind but the beams above their heads would protect them. Nonetheless, she prayed also for luck. For some reason she pictured the Tohunga's whare. Where would he be now? It seemed impossible and yet she had the distinct notion that he was alive, inside that small dwelling of his. No one, she knew for certain, would dare enter the traditional home of a Tohunga. There was no doubt in her mind now, and she did not want to even think of him, except to realise in her own mind that it was he who was responsible, that he alone had ordained this terrible punishment, that on his sanction and his magic, the village and its people were destroyed. The thought made her unhappy. She was not feeling the best and lay down in one corner of the room packed with refugees, her own people and the tourists who had always been good to her and had given her their trust and a genuine friendship. About a third of the room contained pakeha and the rest were mainly women and children from the village. Her thoughts shifted back to Ariki. She had always brought him his food. Give him his due, he had always shown her respect even though he knew that she had a Scottish father. What was the last thing he'd said to her that day? Something about it would be fine for her, what was it?

'I have ordained that you will be safe, Te-Pea Hinerangi, go to your whare when the time comes.'

'Time? I'm not sure what you mean sir.'

'You will find out soon enough. Alright, go now, be careful, note everything and prepare yourself for when Tarawera speaks.'

The roar had not abated, not at all, and she wondered how on this earth she and the folk around her could possibly survive. The old man was right, this was the mountain speaking. She closed her eyes and waited for day, but her heart ached to think what she would see.

*

If the status of Rangatira meant anything at all to Keepa Te-Rangipuawhe it was to help as many people as he could. Despite his great strength and fortitude he was exhausted after shepherding as many as he could into the whare. The never-ending roar of sound dulled his brain as he sat on the bare earth and waited for death. He saw the face of the Tohunga as it was that night after the meeting, ugly in its rage, a seething melt of boiling earth and he knew instinctively what it was that had disturbed the ether, opened the gates of destruction and obliterated forever the place that had been known as TeWairoa. Like McRae he could think of nothing else as the stultifying blackness was interrupted occasionally by the fiery flickering of flame that jiggled and danced through tiny cracks in the walls of the whare, as if the fire was taunting him inside the meeting house and that any minute it would cease its game and burn them to the same white ash that was engulfing the village and the surrounding country.

In that state of mental and physical exhaustion the chief's mind had free rein to wander in a land of waking dreams. Disjointed pictures of the fateful meeting, the Priest's threat, the orange wall of flame then the white hot cones reaching up to the sky. There was no solution to this, no magic that would take it all back so that he would waken from this bad dream and find everyone safe, happy, and the old man ranting as usual.

He lay down. The earth was hot and he felt the weakness sucking him into that area of darkness. But now his daughter's face came to him. She looked at him, through him, at some dream that was slipping away, and he knew this one last thing, this one last duty to perform for her, only for her and he rose up in the last of his great strength, and blundered out into the night.

FIFTEEN

The Tale of William Patton.
Three months earlier

William had come from the industrial county of Yorkshire in the heart of England. He owned a large cotton mill that exported his garments to all parts of the world and had decided to visit New Zealand, encouraged several times by his friend, John Milner, who managed Patton Cotton Spinning and Weaving Industries.

William had read some interesting articles in magazines and the newspapers and seen pictures of what the press referred to as 'the pink and white terraces.' The photographs showed what looked like large circular pools of water descending in giant steps down to a lake. The sheer size of the structure was breathtaking but what really fascinated him was the quality of the waters inside the hot pools. An article in Britain's foremost medical journal, The Lancet, stated that, '…waters, emanating from deep within the earth and forced towards the surface, stemming from a benevolent volcanic activity, possess certain mineral salts that contain curative powers in the healing of muscle, bone and skin disorders.' Not that he had any of those but apparently the water also contained silica salts that improved the tone of the skin.

'No doubt about it William. You just *have* to see this place, it's called, Wao…airoa. I'm not sure about the pronunciation but just ask for the pink and white terraces, everyone knows the terraces.' John had also brought into the office some coloured prints of famous painters who had visited New Zealand. The paintings were apparently true representations of the pink and white terraces. They had discussed the painting and decided that the artist was true to what he saw without any addition to the colours. The painting of the white terraces, showing walls of sinter sparkling in the sun and enclosing pools of warm water reflected blue from the sky, was hard to resist.

His friend accompanied William on the train to Tilbury docks to farewell the 'intrepid' traveller. They were both in high spirits as William was about to become a speck of earth in a vast ocean, comfortably lost inside the iron steam-ship that took up most of the wharf. The band played alongside the ship as confetti and coloured streamers thrown onto the dock from the lower and upper decks of the ship gave a festive air to their departure.

'If I didn't have so much work on I would have come with you my friend. Go on, have a great time there, perfect place for a single man, the land of adventure, lots of beer, native girls, the lot. You won't know yourself, probably come back here with a Maori lady, you'll be a sensation.'

'Some hopes. Maori lady indeed, fat chance *I've* got!' William was of average height, tending slightly to plumpness from muscles that had become strangers to exercise. His hands, unlike the rough, hard, sinewy palms of his workers, were by contrast soft, totally unused to labour apart from pushing a pen across paper or lifting the odd glass of ale in the pub. The man's compassion showed in his face, and his pleasant blue eyes were set in pink cheeks that contrasted with a pale skin that had lost its acquaintance with the sun. He was friendly and kind to all his staff, and every Christmas the office and factory workers enjoyed a substantial bonus. The affable exterior hid a shrewd understanding of people and of business that had enabled him to build one of the most productive cotton spinning factories in England.

The band was playing some of Elgar's famous marches as the latest sea-going craft, part of the new generation of iron steamships, slowly peeled away from the wharf and within five minutes John's face disappeared among the fading crowd as they pulled out into the English Channel. From there they steamed into the Atlantic, heading towards the blue waters of the Southern ocean, via the azure Mediterranean and finally the Pacific and New Zealand.

By the time the 'Stadt Harlem' berthed in the small port of Tauranga, William, sea-hardened, walked out onto the dock having to re-establish his land legs.

The journey took him about three days from Tauranga, having stopped first at Rotorua before the final and shorter journey to Te Wairoa. If the wonders of Rotorua were anything to go by the thought of the pink and white terraces was something he could hardly wait to see. He had been to Bath and 'taken the waters,' but Rotorua and its massive boiling-mud pools, its relaxing hot pools amidst the trees, was in a different league compared to the rather tepid waters of Bath.

*

On William's second day in Te Wairoa he was in his element. It had been a wonder and a revelation for the cotton spinning and weaving factory owner to see the great terraces. To actually bathe in them, whenever he chose, exceeded his wildest expectations. Where would you ever see such beauty anywhere on this earth? How warm the water was, the walls of pure silica with sparkling sinter that glistened like jewels in the sun. Apart from the beauty of the white terrace, he was fascinated by its transparency. At times he would fall sleep and when he woke up it felt like he was sitting in the open with no water at all and he had to move his body to see tiny ripples across the surface.

*

The Maori woman was in his reckoning about twenty five at the most. She walked with a grace and elegance that gave her an air of authority. Her jet black hair sparkled in the sun, taking on at times a deep purple tinge. She removed her cloak of woven flax decorated here and there with the brown speckled feathers of a bird, giving it to an elderly woman who had accompanied her and appeared to be a chaperone. William was bathing alone, as he had been for two days. The water was at its best in the central part of the complex, warm and relaxing. The terraced pools ascended in giant steps towards the massive aperture at the summit, where boiling water from deep below ground flowed into the basins, gradually cooling before reaching the lake.

The young lady made her way towards the centre of the terraces and he had the distinct notion that she might just make it to where he was bathing. The next moment she climbed over, seemingly to join William, and sat down, flexing her arms and legs back and forth in the relaxing warmth of the spring.

Her light brown skin glowed and with her eyes closed she sank into the warmth of the pool. William could hardly take his eyes off her when she suddenly looked up, directly into his face. He would have turned away but her lips parted in the most charming smile. The smile was the prelude to her voice. 'Excuse me. Did you know that you can rest your arms on the sinter walls, like this.' She spread both her arms out in a relaxing position on top of the glistening walls of sinter that enclosed the pool. 'See? Is that more comfortable?' She had the accent typical of her race, yet her English was very good. She spoke matter-of-factly, her voice down to earth.

'Oh!' The sudden practical nature of her suggestion surprised William. 'Well, yes but I thought they might be, you know, hard.'

'Hard?' She laughed politely. To William's surprise she eased over to him. Taking his arm in one hand she placed it over the top. 'There. How does that feel?'

'It's fine. Surprising, it's actually very soft and it seems to give, like a pillow.'

'Of course. 'You were missing the fun sitting the way you were. The walls are soft, very soft.'

William had no time to think. He wanted to say it was very nice, that he had never had any woman ever do that for him, or that he had rarely, no, *never* seen anyone with her natural beauty coupled with an ability to put another human being completely at their ease. He remembered reading that one of the main characteristics of a civilized person was just that. The ability to make their fellow humans safe and comfortable.

'Thank you. This certainly feels a lot better. And I was thinking they would be sharp.'

'Because of the sparkles? Many visitors think that at first. They imagine the sparkling bits in the wall are like glass. Quite the opposite. Look.'

She rubbed her hand and small particles of sinter came away. She showed it to him, palm up.

She was the most unaffected person he had ever met, and conversation with her was easy and interesting. He asked her how she spoke such good English and she told him that her father was the Rangatira, the head of her tribe and he had sent her to a convent in Tauranga for her education.

The afternoon drifted on towards early evening. They talked for some of the time and relaxed in between. Uncertain of her reaction, he asked whether they could meet tomorrow and was delighted when she agreed and said she would look forward to it.

*

William had arrived two weeks before Tarawera mountain was rent asunder in one of the most violent eruptions of all time. Herena had taken him to meet her father, Keepa Te-Rangipuawhe, who was very impressed that his daughter had befriended this cheerful, humble man, yet one who owned a vast factory in England that made clothes for people, 'all over the world,' his daughter had stressed. He was even more impressed when he saw the young man in McRae's tavern drinking not alcohol, but a pot of tea, with sandwiches. Of course he would never entertain the idea of Herena going anywhere near the tavern. She and William had travelled through the district, seeing everything there was to see with Herena acting as a willing and enthusiastic guide. The Rangatira suspected that they were in love and the thought didn't seem at all to perturb him. Herena had been well educated and the daughter of a chieftain deserved the best that life had to offer. But that best was now in question and the prospect troubled him. The Tohunga's rage, at the meeting, contained dire warnings of the mountain's wrath and the recent accumulation of minor shakes were harbingers of an uncertain future. So much the better then if his daughter were out of it, away in a foreign land with a fine young man who owned a factory that employed hundreds of people, a good man whose humility and self-discipline had impressed him.

The Rangatira was right to be concerned. While the relationship between his beautiful daughter and her humble Englishman was unfolding, far below the earth forces that were hostile to men, that understood their weak mortality, were about to inflict unimaginable suffering upon those mortals that lived below the shadow of Tarawera mountain and would alter forever their transient existence in the place where great happiness, beauty and joy had prevailed. A priest had performed his ritual, given his sanction, and out of a faultlessly clear night sky the mountain would answer.

*

For William Patton the prospect of wandering in an angry red darkness with a mountain raging above him would have been too horrific, too impossible for him to consider, yet here, in this absolute blackness, with shards of scoria raining down on him, he could only think of Herena and where she would be at this time. He tried to call her name, turning his face into a threatening sky, and his rasping croak was swallowed into the dark wind.

Four successive blasts of white-hot lava, powering thousands of feet into the sky, had transformed the landscape into a dark, surreal red. He tried again and again, finally hearing his own voice, a faint whisper against the persistent roar of Tarawera but clear nonetheless, against the fractured sky. A splinter struck him on his head and he fell, dazed, but the strike only made him more than ever determined to find her–his prize, the greatest find of his life and he was not prepared to falter.

It did not occur to the wealthy owner of a cotton factory in middle England, who found himself staggering through a mire of ash and a rain of fiery fragments, that life was unfair, that he did not deserve this. In a land that he knew nothing of, he knew only that he had to find a woman, to save her and keep her safe. But he was finding it harder and harder to continue and he fell into a mound of debris. Lying against jagged stones that stung his face and hands, the thought came to him that he could die very soon.

The acrid stench of superheated air coming down from the mountain clogged his throat and burnt his nostrils.

It had become impossible to give in, not now. They had agreed to meet so she had to be somewhere here, somewhere. Successive blasts of blistering wind threw fragments of earth and scoria into his face. He would take whatever the mountain would throw at him, and he shouted her name again and again, reeling in the swamp of volcanic wreckage, a minute speck of humanity, undefeated by a raging mountain, lost in the turmoil of what had yesterday been the most beautiful place on this earth. By this time he knew he was not going to make it to safety.

A powerful hand stretched out in the darkness. It drew him in and he heard the deep voice of the Rangatira, Keepa Te-Rangipuawhe the father of his beloved Herena, calling his name. 'William! Is it really you out here? I've been doing what I can to help. I was about to go back then I heard you calling the name of my daughter. Come with me son. In this night of horror you have actually faced death itself in the hope of saving Herena.' There was an urgency in Keepa's voice. 'Come on, you are the last person I've seen here, the rest are in the whare. With Maui's help we shall see this terrible night through.'

Despite his own suffering the Rangatira smiled in admiration to hear the Englishman's reply, through the successive blasts of hot air loaded with dust and razor-edged splinters of rock. The young man was hardly able to speak at all. 'Sir, she sho…should have met me today. I can't…can't…leave until we find her. She…'

They were shouting through the storm, the words disjointed against the roar of the mountain. 'But Herena *is* safe, William. I had to stop her from doing the same thing as yourself. She shelters in the whare and I know she waits for you.' In the turmoil that raged and buffeted the two men, William saw reassurance in the large warrior face of the chief, and he felt the shock of sweet relief. The chief had him by the shoulders, his massive body a stone against the flood, and William felt himself pulled, half dragged to safety, to where his lovely Herena waited with an anxiety and a dread not for herself but for him.

SIXTEEN

Rapata and Kaheru reached Tauranga the following afternoon after their arrival at Rotorua. The sadness of leaving her father and mother had been eased, firstly by her parent's own choice to stay in Te Wairoa and then knowing that she was with Rapata. That which they would encounter together was to come in their lives. At no time had she asked him to explain what had happened between himself and the great Tohunga, knowing full well the tapu that would be involved if he were to reveal this thing. His manner had suggested clearly, both to her and her father Hunapo, that it would be very bad for them to stay in the village. They had looked after the group well and the tourists had been more than kind by taking them to Tauranga. They had enjoyed the sight of the young people's wonder and manifest pleasure at seeing Tauranga for the first time in their lives. In the few days that they had been together, Inger Lindau had forged a deep friendship with Kaheru who had been quick to learn words and sometimes whole sentences in English. The men quizzed Rapata about his life and in his guide's English he was able to brief them on life and customs in the village.

'We leave by ship tomorrow,' one of the men told them. 'I'll disembark in Auckland and these people will continue their journey to Sweden. There's a small lodging just opposite the dock. Stay there for tonight then you can see us off in the afternoon.'

The man's name was Larsen, and he introduced them to the manager of a ferry service that operated across the harbour to neighbouring towns on the coast. 'He's a ferryman, big strong feller. Do you have anything for him here Bill?'

Bill Franklyn looked Rapata up and down. He seemed pleased. 'Just the type of chap I need, he'll soon learn the ropes. Speaks more than a bit of English too. I'll start him next week. They can live here.'

Both men shook hands and it was done.

*

Kaheru knew that her Rapata had read the signs well. This was more than they had possibly hoped for. At night she lay awake in wonder at how their lives were being improved since their flight from Te Wairoa. It was then that she thought about the Tohunga. He had advised his ferryman to leave, telling him to go as far as possible. It followed then that the Tohunga's influence had caused this to happen. Yes. She was certain the priest's blessings had followed Rapata. Thanks from such a man had far-reaching consequences, and she was grateful. Then the thought settled in her mind, so did his displeasure with the land that had been her home since birth, and she waited for what that would be.

In his dream Rapata was ferrying the old man across the lake. The Priest was standing at the prow as the canoe hissed through the placid water. A dark cloud appeared above their heads followed by a wind gusting in from the mountain. The boat heaved across the tumult, and he strove to keep it level as the wind picked up and changed into a storm. Scarlet lightning raced across the sky, followed by deafening thunder. The old man held his position as the craft reeled and bucked against a massive wall of waves that poured in relentlessly to overturn the craft. Rain stung his face and the stench of sulphur rose from the lake as Rapata shouted through the storm, warning Tuhoto of the danger, advising him to sit down. The old man turned, his face unmoved as he stared at the ferryman. *'No Rapata, your danger is past. Wake, witness my power, and what you have fled.'*

It was dark in the small room that was near to the dock. He stood up, feeling the ground shake, and gently stirred Kaheru from sleep.

'Rapata, what…' The sound of distant thunder and flashes of lightning against the horizon interrupted her.

'The Tohunga, he was in my dream.' They walked to the front door and again felt the ground shake beneath them. Kaheru held his arm to stop herself from falling as they walked outside. The lightning was far off and they heard a distant thunder, rapid detonations one after another, then more lightning.

'This is not a storm, Rapata.' She pointed to the direction of the sounds and where the sky glowed, pulsating with a fierce intensity across the horizon.

Rapata stood behind her with his arms wrapped round her shoulders. 'We know where it is.'

She shook her head and was silent.

'The Tohunga spoke when we were in the boat. He said that my danger had passed, but that I should witness what we have left behind.'

'I believe it.' She turned, looking up into his face, her eyes large, trusting and reflecting the red of the distant sky. 'The priest saved us. But I fear for my family.'

'Do not fear. If he told me of the danger beforehand and what I must do, maybe he will ordain that they too are well. Your father Hunapo and your mother chose to stay, wait and see.'

They were at the dockside by mid-afternoon to say goodbye to their friends of the last two days. The tourists and all the town's people had seen the red sky in the distance and heard distant thunder and lightning. By daybreak they had been informed of the massive explosion at Tarawera. It became clear to Inger why Rapata had warned her of danger, back in Rotorua. How had he known? She had seen the absolute beauty of his village, there was nothing like it in Sweden, probably the whole earth, but now this element of mystery, a warning from the young man. Her heart ached for what she knew now would be the destruction of his village and all that incredible beauty. But it lived in her mind and there it would stay all her life.

Mr Larsen saw him before they sailed for Auckland and told Rapata that he actually owned the ferry service and that he came down once or twice a year to Tauranga. 'I'll see you then Rapata and you Miss Kaheru. We've enjoyed having you both on the trip.' Larsen had found their honesty and integrity

126

refreshing after all the petty haggling and money-grabbing at Te Wairoa. There must have been many like these two, just that he hadn't met them. He knew also that if the mountain had blown, they would have no home to return to. He never mentioned this to the others but they would have felt the same and he felt good about his decision.

Inger hugged Kaheru and she in turn showed her how to rub noses in the traditional manner of a Maori farewell. She stood on deck, the last one to remain as the steamship pulled away. She would always remember them standing together, dressed not in western clothes but the graceful traditional Maori cloaks woven out of flax, each with a cape of brown and white feathers, and waving politely from the dock.

Maybe she would come back to New Zealand after all.

SEVENTEEN

The port at Tauranga was busy with passengers travelling overnight to Auckland and from there making the five week journey to England. Keepa, wearing the traditional robe of his status as Rangatira of the district, was saying goodbye to his daughter and her husband.

Travellers leaving Aotearoa, the land they knew as New Zealand, thought the young man and woman standing on the dockside must be special people to have the small imposing assembly of Maori dignitaries, men and women who had the stamp of warriorship, perform a short but moving farewell ceremony. Keepa Te-Rangipuawhe spoke in English, his words translated for the group of ten officials by the recently appointed assistant director of operations for what remained of his village.

'You have come to us at the right time William. When I found you in that night of great horror, one step removed from death but determined to seek and find my daughter, I saw the actions of a very brave and caring man. Love such as that is eternal. Go with the blessing of myself and of our people. You will return when things have settled here.'

*

On the opposite side of the earth, far removed from the white heat and the havoc of Tarawera, on a typically autumn day, England was enjoying the last of an Indian summer. John Milner saw two people emerge through the frontiers of white uniformed men coldly examining documents and papers before their entrance into normalcy and England. He noted a young woman of great beauty with hair that swept in a jet-black shine down to her waist. The woman stood out among the crowd; he thought she would stand out anywhere. A man was with her who showed some papers to the authorities. The omnipotent guardians of Britain, seated at heavy oak desks, looked carefully at the documents then up at the young woman. The man with her was explaining something to the white uniformed official who was finding it hard not to stare at the lady in question. The officer seemed very taken with the young woman then he smiled, stamped her documents and motioned that she could pass unhindered into England.

John realised that the man with her was– William! A William that at first he hadn't recognized. The same looks, the same face, but not the same man who had left these shores five months previously. It was his business as factory manager to read people and he realised then it was something inside his friend that had changed. A sort of metamorphosis had occurred within the man and he knew without a doubt that it was to do with the beautiful woman walking straight and erect at his side. John Milner smiled wryly at his own prophecy, at the time delivered half in jest. *'You won't know yourself, probably come back here with a Maori lady, you'll be a sensation.'*

They walked towards him and he stretched out his hand to greet the lady but she ignored it, leaned forward, then gently holding his shoulders the Maori noblewoman rubbed noses with the Englishman.

'It's the way they do things out there, John.'

'I'm not complaining William.'

EIGHTEEN

SIC TRANSIT GLORIA MUNDI

The space was in absolute blackness. All matter came from blackness and in that dark matter of the universe was fashioned the genesis of creation. The mountain had destroyed absolutely what he had deemed to be destroyed and, in the fire of purification, the tapu of what had been placed upon the land was removed. The beauty that had in time corrupted his land was now stripped bare beneath its coverlet of volcanic ash.

In this absolute darkness there was nothing, the perfection of nothing and he could feel only the earth beneath his invisible feet. The mountain had spared him; spared his legs, his body, his arms and his eyes. Legs that would stand, eyes that would see the final cleansing of the land. He had given the mountain sanction to cleanse that which had been violated. There was in the Tohunga's mind no doubt and his mind was as clear as had been the crystal water, the shining sinter that illuminated the banks of pure marble and the absolute clarity of the lake. Nothing lasts, and the mountain had spoken in the act of fire. In time, fire would generate the destruction of the earth. By then all things would have become defiled, polluted by men, corrupted by their unbounded desire for the illusion of wealth of abundance that existed only in their minds.

Aporo Te Wharekaniwha had imagined that abundance lay in the amount of small, metal coins and he had placed them in the eyes of the gods, by whose sacred and inviolate ordinance the tribe had been governed. That night at the meeting he had revealed to his tribe the abundance of the land. That which was far removed from the spurious wealth of the pakeha, their tin coins, their liquor that made sterile the strength of his warriors so that they reeled, vomited, fell to the ground in shameful stupors and were either laughed at or else joined by the pakehas.

Aporo and the elders of his tribe were blind to the riches he had indicated that night. They had not seen the wealth that those same gods had provided: the abundance of the trees, the fruits, the glistening jewels of dew that clung to the totara leaves and the petals of yellow kowhai. The great gift of the waters warmed by Maui himself so his people could see his profusion of gifts bestowed upon the Te Arawa. At first their innocence had been rewarded ten-fold, but then they had spat in the face of the gods. As night follows day, it had now become the work of the Tohunga to be the instrument of Maui and in his name he had wreaked his vengeance upon the tribe.

Summoning the powers bequeathed to him according to the sacred traditions of his ministry, he had placed the matae atua upon the head of the chief of Ngati Hinemihi. Inexorably his curse was followed by death. Tuhoto understood the dynamic power of such a curse, knew also that should a curse of such magnitude be placed upon one who was blameless or undeserving, it would fall upon his own head and he

132

would weaken and die. Only a Tohunga with great power could place such a curse on the head of a tribal chief and warrior, else it would be rendered ineffective and his tribe would laugh at him. Neither of these alternatives bothered him.

He had known all along of Aporo's fate just as he knew and understood the infinite mechanics of the universe. Aporo Te Wharekaniwha had died but the spirit that was once Chief of Ngati Hinemihi would be spared its own hell of eternal wandering. Aporo had, at the last moment, seen and understood the serious nature of the hara he had committed and why the matae atua had followed. In his realisation came final atonement and salvation.

There was now an absolute certainty in his mind about the justice of what had taken place. Te Tarata and Otukapuarangi had been seized in the hand of Maui, crushed and taken below the lake, out of sight from his people, from the pakeha, who would come and see—nothing. The mountain had been rent in two and even in this all-consuming blackness, he knew how it was outside his whare. Their world covered in ash, in the white of purification. The scorched earth, the trees, the water, the entire marks of their habitation rendered white. Pure, cleansed—white…white…white. Tuhoto breathed deeply and emptied his mind into the absolute quiet of cosmic awareness.

*

Day, night, day, night, day. Small sounds, sifting through the absolute silence, penetrating the dark, interrupting his meditation, and now muffled human voices brought the Tohunga from out of the cosmic field.

He cleared his throat and spoke but nothing came from his mouth. Reaching out he felt the pitcher of water, still there from the ministrations of the guide, Te-Pea Hinerangi. He spoke again and again until at last the words came, words that told whoever it was that he chose to remain here in the dark, words that told his rescuers there was no need for his rescue. Yet the voices persisted and he could even hear their speech, pakeha speech, and he wanted none of it. He had spoken in Maori and of course they did not understand. There would be none of his tribe to interpret and in the dark he smiled to himself. Those who had not perished would flee and their fear of him would be too great to endure his presence or for them even to behold his countenance.

The voices became clearer. He told them to go and save the others, seek Te-Pea Hinerangi. In the darkness he spat in disgust realizing they probably didn't know her by that name. He knew she would be safe. Safe too any pakeha or Maori who had sheltered with her. The sound of human voices outside his whare persisted and he wanted the people to leave, there was nothing here for them except the darkness, it was not for them.

*

A rescue party of volunteers had been assigned to dig out the ash that had solidified and they were astonished to hear a voice inside of what definitely looked like a dwelling under a heavy blanket of white residue. They were unable to fathom what the man was saying. No Maori would come hear the place now and the rescue party, designated by the council, had been briefed about this by the officials. The governor had appointed his representative who had anticipated the problem beforehand. 'We've sent over someone who speaks Maori, Sir. I hear he's an educated man.'

'Good, excellent. Does he...you know, believe in this tapu business?'

The representative was in his fifties. He had the face of a man used to command, lined with the rigors of office and in most cases getting his way in matters official. 'Probably not, Sir. He's aware of the tapu practiced by his people, of course, but I don't think that he actually believes in it, if you follow.'

'Yes I do and be thankful for that. He'll be a great help to us. We have to get people out of there. What's his name?'

'Leni Sir, Leni Franklyn.'

'Well he can be part of the rescue team.'

Leni Franklyn, the man in question, could understand Maori perfectly as his mother had been Maori and his father English. He had been sent to England to study and had done very well. The governor had quizzed one or two of the officials who would oversee rescue efforts at Te Wairoa. From what they had seen it was possible to rectify the damage in Rotorua. Te Wairoa would take a lot longer, perhaps forever.

Leni was working with a group of men some distance from the whare of the Tohunga when he was called over by Jack Taylor, a council official in charge of rescue operations. Jack understood that Leni had been sent in with a team from Tauranga, by the governor, who had instigated the rescue and wanted a direct report back as soon as possible on the state of the settlement and surrounding areas.

'Leni, I'm glad you're here. Look, we're having a problem. We have a bloke inside here.' Jack Taylor indicated a small dwelling with a load of ash on top of the roof. 'Would you believe it, he doesn't sound too happy to see us.'

Leni grinned and moving on hands and knees looked through a small aperture into the darkness of the dwelling. Waiting for his eyes to settle for a few seconds he saw an old man sitting on the floor. The man looked at him and asked who he was. He seemed, if not pleased, relieved to hear someone speak in Maori.

'We've come to rescue you.'

'Go away.'

'My name is Leni.' He thought it a good idea not to mention his last name.

'Leni, tell the pakeha to go, I have no wish to see them. This is my village and I come out when I'm ready.'

The village was a blanket of dirty white that had settled across the land, across the dwellings and the ruins, resembling a solidified, multi layered cake.

'Yes of course. I understand fully. But there is nothing here, it's all been destroyed, the volcano has…'

'Do you think I do not know what the volcano has done? I know what has happened. I knew it long before you came here.' The old man looked at Leni and the would-be rescuer noted the authority in his face. 'Who do you think brought this destruction here? I am Tuhoto Ariki. The Tohunga of Te Arawa. I know exactly what is here and what is not here.'

Leni was shocked. He stepped back and looked at Jack Taylor who had been watching the conversation.

'Having trouble?' Jack laughed. 'I told you, the old chap doesn't want to come out.'

Leni looked thoughtful. 'Yes, we have something of a dilemma here. I've heard all about him. He's a Tohunga. The others are frightened of him.' He looked at Jack, his face serious. 'Apparently he is the one who placed a curse on his tribe.' He looked around outside, remembering how it had been. He knew Jack had seen TeWairoa before, so had he, and it pained him to see the absolute destruction of what he had always thought of as a natural and remarkable showpiece that would rank with any on the earth. 'They believe that he caused it. They say he had placed a curse on the tribe for the corruption that had come about here. You see I spoke to some of his people before this, just to get some idea of what was happening. Strange how he's still alive.'

Jack looked thoughtful for a moment then he looked inside again. The Tohunga was sitting down and seemed at peace. 'You did absolutely right of course. However that doesn't alter the fact that it's still my job to get the feller out. We've no time for all that ruddy superstitious nonsense. Right?'

Leni looked at the man in charge of operations. Hell of a job, glad he wasn't in charge. Jack's face and arms were slightly sunburnt from hours spent in the open.

'Okay, I'll do my best to get the old chap out then.'

He eventually coaxed the old man into leaving his whare. He called him 'sir' and apologized for their presence and the Tohunga seemed pleased with that. Both the rescuers were fascinated by the man. He was tall, very tall. His lean frame and his manner had that bearing typical of a man of power and something else that Jack Taylor could not quite place. Some innate quality that in his experience of men was new to him. He decided to let Leni do the work of somehow convincing the man that he could not stay here, that all of his people were to be relocated. He had gathered, in consultation with the council officials in Tauranga, that it would be somewhere in Rotorua.

Leni waited patiently, standing behind the Tohunga as the priest inspected the remains of the village, the lake and the vast blanket of whitened ash that despoiled the once beautiful frontiers of Te Wairoa. He thought that the Tohunga seemed to be at peace, with no signs of loss or regret like he had seen in those inhabitants who had escaped the disaster.

A thin wind blew across the desert lifting some white dust, pressing his cloak against the tall, gaunt frame. In the distance a water bird flew across the ashen, soupy water of the lake, then at the last minute it peeled away as though in disgust and gaining height headed north for cleaner water.

The Tohunga walked forwards a few paces. The entire landscape had changed since the massive eruption of the mountain. The creature inside the mountain had exerted its destructive power to follow his command. Its reward was that it would be set free, its thousand-year exile was over and it could no longer live in the mountain. Without the great spirit inside its depths Tarawera mountain would sleep for another thousand years.

Tuhoto Ariki turned, seeing the man who had introduced himself as Leni. A nice fellow, who understood him and was respectful.

'Leni. Your name means the graciousness of god. It is a good omen.' He pointed to the sea of ash and mud covering the entire landscape. 'The trees will grow again and the grasses will come back to the land.' The punishment of his tribe had been absolute but he did not speak of this to the young man. 'So, Leni, where are they taking me?'

'Oh I'm not sure sir. I have heard that you will be relocated in Rotorua somewhere.'

'Who has arranged this?'

'Well I believe it was the authorities.'

'They know nothing of what has passed between me and my people. Those in Rotorua will not see me. My presence to them will be tapu. So too is this place.' He lifted his hand indicating the village, buried in the white ash of the mountain. 'They have deemed it as tapu,' he explained. 'Of course they know nothing. It *was* tapu because of the men's violation of our sacred laws, but now it has been cleansed. In time it will improve, and to live here would be like the great days of my tribe's honour and warriorship of the

Te Arawa. They know nothing of the fires of purification.'

Leni let the Tohunga speak. He found it fascinating and everything the man said seemed to resonate in a long-lost part of his being, educated as he was in England. Strangely he believed him, unlike the 'superstitious nonsense' that Jack had called it. Yet he could see that Jack had been impressed with the man.

'Sir.'

The Tohunga turned and the deep fierce eyes studied him.

'Sir, I need to go and see some people, like the men who found you. Then I will be back, is that all right?'

The priest's face softened and he laughed good-humouredly at the young man's concern. He was reminded of Rapata and he was glad that the ferryman was safe.

'I have been under the ground for three days, protected by the very mountain that destroyed everything. And you ask if I will be safe?'

He indicated that Leni should leave. 'Come back if you want or leave me here. It matters not at all.'

It took Leni half an hour to find the rescue and search party. There was one guide with them, a man who had lived here, less superstitious than his people. Leni spoke to him in Maori.

'You appear to be the only one from your tribe prepared to help out here. What is your name, if I may ask?'

'Hunapo. I did live here and was saved by sheltering in the whare of our guide, Te-Pea Hinerangi.'

'That was fortunate but what about...I mean are you married, children? Are they alright?'

'Thanks for asking. Yes we were lucky that Te-Pea took us all in.'

Leni told him how they had discovered the old Tohunga, Tuhoto Ariki.

Hunapo thought long and hard before he answered. 'Then he was protected. It was his curse upon us that sent the gods of destruction.' He looked into the white ash covering everything for miles, the remnants of the lake, a sea of milk. 'Yes, of course. Rapata knew this, he knew but could not tell. I see now that the Tohunga would have warned him to leave and in so doing, saved him and my daughter.'

The man spoke as though to himself and whatever it was, Leni saw plainly a certain relief on his face.

'Yes, the thing is Mr Hunapo, we have to relocate you all. The question is, what about your Tohunga?'

'The Tohunga, like the rest of this place, is absolutely tapu to my people. To even look at him, to discuss him, is to invite disaster. They will never return here. This ground is tapu, forever.' He smiled at Leni. 'I am not sure where the government will send us but wherever it is, you or those in charge will have to take the Tohunga somewhere else. I assure you no one, no one, will want to see him again or even think of him.'

'What about you? Do you believe he is tapu, that this place is tapu?'

'What I think doesn't matter. All I know is that I am safe and so is my wife. We have been spared. My daughter left some time back, with her husband. To answer your question about tapu, yes I believe that certain things are not for us in this world, that they would harm us and we cannot understand them. Personally, I do not regard either the Tohunga or this place as tapu, not now.'

Leni was very interested in this man. The first man he had met from the village as the rest had left and would never return. 'I believe you. The Tohunga told me what he had done. He said the village had become corrupted and…'

'There he was right. Yes it had become corrupted, of course. The pakeha had lavished their money on us and most of the tribe neither understood nor were they able to deal with the sudden wealth.' He looked up at Leni, speaking matter-of-factly, and shrugged. 'The pakeha were good people, they meant well but we were too innocent. We did not understand about these things.'

Hunapo did not elaborate and Leni had learned a lot talking to him. 'Well, I thank you for your kindness and wish you all the best with your family.' He looked around at the desolation that surrounded them. 'I will get back to the others. We have to make some decisions here and there's a lot of work to be done.'

'I also have much to do Mr. Franklyn. Good luck in your work.' Hunapo walked back to his own group to help with excavations. He turned, and a wry smile broke out across his affable face, his head and shoulders white with dust. 'And do *you* believe what the Tohunga said, about Tarawera?'

Leni was walking back to where he had left Tuhoto. 'I found it hard to believe at first, but maybe events on this earth *can* be influenced by us. Anyway back to the man who, in that case, has awakened the volcano. He has been admitted to the hospital for a check-up. So I was told.' He walked back to the nothing that was the village with its sole inhabitant.

'Whether he'll stay there is another thing.'

*

After three days at the hospital Tuhoto Ariki had had enough. He had eaten none of their food, regarding it as tapu. He left the establishment in the early dawn on the third day, unnoticed by the staff. Frank Taylor was informed by a rather irritated Governor's representative. 'Yes. Gone. Ungrateful if you ask me, considering we looked after him. Of course the obdurate fellow wouldn't eat a scrap of food. Said it was …Oh now what's the word tap… something?'

'That's tapu, Sir.'

Oh well, look, you'd better find the fellow. I don't want us to be blamed for…'

'I'll get our man Leni, Sir, Leni Franklyn.'

'Yes, do that, please.'

Leni Franklyn studied the tall figure of the priest. The old man had left the hospital, disgusted with the doctors, nurses and the entire staff, outraged

143

that they had cut his hair. 'Tidied him up,' were the words used by the government agent.

Ariki had walked back to his village and Leni had found him there looking out across the blanket of white ash; all that remained of Te Wairoa. The priest's eyes looked out across the absolute desolation of what had once been the lake, with its many tributaries reaching out to the great terraces.

'All their gold, the greed of those who were corrupted by the Pakeha, buried. Before the coming of the Pakeha my people were blameless.'

The old man's eyes rested on Leni Franklyn, as though seeing him for the first time.

'I am glad you are here.' He pointed towards a small knoll covered in volcanic ash, then stretched his hand out towards Leni. The priest's face revealed the construction of his mind and the finality of the moment was not lost on Leni. Ariki's hand was cold, his body wasted from days of fasting and refusing all food offered by the hospital. Helped by Leni he reached the top of the knoll. The eyes, that had once blazed across that which he saw as the tapu of his tribe, were suddenly in another place, far removed from this desolate present.

A thin wind stirred across the wasteland forming a small vortex of ash, then died away. The priest sat down, his upper body leaning back against the shoulder of the mound. He spoke a few words as though in prayer, then he motioned the young man to come closer. *'I was the agent. My duty was to cleanse that which had been corrupted. There was no malice in my action. I did what was ordained and it is over.'*

144

He looked once at Leni before his eyes closed, followed by a long breath that rasped across the wind, then there was nothing. Frank waited, feeling the death clutch of his hand, placing it against the side of the priest. He stayed there for some time then walked down the slope. He decided he would get Jack Taylor to remove the priest's body. He had walked for a hundred yards or so when he looked back. A few swirls of ash appeared to move around the body as though in some blind attempt to cover it. Jack would inform the Governor's agent and they could decide on the burial of the Tohunga. For certain no Maori would dare touch or even look at the body now.

NINETEEN

Leni Franklyn had been promoted by the governor's agent as the advisor for the massive clean-up and rescue of what was left of Te Wairoa. Part of his brief was to administer the stay of Tuhoto in the hospital and the decision concerning the burial rites for a Tohunga.

He had tried his best to get the people living in the area to undertake the burial of the Tohunga but they hardly wanted to acknowledge his existence, let alone discuss such a thing. Requests and enquiries in Rotorua and up to the far north met with the same response. The interment of Tuhoto's body would be a desecration of Maori burial ground. Apart from anything else, cutting the Tohunga's hair during his brief spell in hospital was an unspeakable act and a supreme violation of tapu.

Unable to make any progress, he reported back to the official. 'Sir, neither heaven nor hell will move my people to even mention his name anymore. He is considered absolutely tapu by the entire tribe of the Te Arawa. As for undertaking his burial rites according to the traditions of Maoridom, well that remains in the realms of impossibility. Did you know that the entire village of Te Wairoa has been designated as tapu?'

'No, I didn't. I don't suppose that will remain for long though, will it? I mean people are curious, once the dust settles.' The agent looked apologetically at Leni and tapped his forehead. 'Excuse my unfortunate choice of metaphor but you know what I mean. What I was going to say was that tourism is bound to take over, now and in the years to come. What do you think?' He knew that Leni was a sensible man, part-Maori, part-pakeha, a civil engineer, trained in Britain and respected by the local Maori and by the English for his services to the local Iwi and to the crown, so he was interested in the man's reply.

'Eventually it will, although how long the memory of Tuhoto will persist in remaining tapu, who can say? In Maori culture the Tohunga is a priest both feared and respected, and in Tuhoto's case you can put "feared" first.'

The agent representing the governor looked thoughtful as Leni continued.

'You see they blame him entirely for this tragedy. But in essence Tuhoto's dissatisfaction with the way the people of Te Wairoa were absorbing western culture displeased him and his curse apparently can disturb the forces of nature. Enough, my people believe, to cause the eruption.'

'Yes I understand all that but personally I am not interested in the metaphysics of this or any other event. To say that an ancient priest can upset the balance of nature is frankly preposterous. Nature,' explained the official, pointing towards the ceiling, 'is unassailable. Unaffected and indifferent to human beliefs. If indeed nature did have a voice it would laugh at all this superstition, and allow me to point out that metaphysics, in my humble opinion, is just a lot of damn poppycock.'

147

Having clarified the true nature of events in the tragedy, he looked up at the large painting of the Tohunga on the wall to one side of the oak desk that traditionally was the workplace of the governor. Unconsciously he rearranged a large and very valuable crystal vase to the centre of the desk, a present from the ambassador of Austria who had arrived last year.

'Yes, poor old fella, blamed for everything. Of course people have to blame someone and this chap copped the lot. For heaven's sake, the old man badly needed a haircut. He ought to be grateful that he's had a decent Christian burial, not to mention a damn fine headstone. Well that ought to please the Maoris eh? Their old, er...what's that they call him?'

'Tohunga sir...he's...'

'Yes of course. Anyway that's why I thought it a good idea to appoint you to this post. As you know I can never pronounce these names.'

'The haircut, incidentally was also a very bad idea. You see to the Maori the head of the Tohunga is sacred, inviolate and must never be touched.'

'Good heavens!'

'Yes. Once you cut the man's hair all hell broke loose. They will have nothing to do with the body. In fact wherever he is buried the ground becomes tapu.'

'And what if they hadn't cut his hair?'

A wry smile preceded his answer. 'In this particular case, the same I'm afraid.'

The agent looked down at some letters he had to sign, shaking his head. 'It's one thing after another. We feed the fellow, we clean him up, tidy up all that hair and it's wrong? Oh well never mind. We've done our best.'

Leni could have added that had the Governor, presently in Auckland, and a few of his staff taken the time to learn a few ground rules of Maoridom it might have spared everyone, Maori and English, a lot of grief. Anyway it was all too late. No more pink and white terraces, no more Te Wairoa. That was the real tragedy and nothing was going to bring it back.

*

The governor's representative was asleep in bed that night when he heard a muffled thud downstairs. He got out of bed and pushed open the heavy door of his bedroom. Two oil lamps along the length of the passage cast an orange glow across the hallway, slanting across the curved staircase that led into the study. There was security posted round the spacious building and he had cautioned them about going to sleep on the job. One hand on the balustrade to muffle his footsteps, he moved cautiously down the long curving staircase until he saw that there was no one at all inside the large study. A single night lamp inside the room flickered uneasily inside its glass casing. Apart from the sharp geometric shadows of furniture that danced across walls and carpets, the room was thankfully empty and he saw what it was that had woken him at two am. The painting of the Tohunga, Tuhoto Ariki, had slid off the wall and landed onto the Governor's prized possession, the heavy oak desk shipped over from England. Relieved, he descended the staircase and walked over to the desk. As he picked up the heavy oil painting of the Tohunga he

149

cursed under his breath on seeing the deep gouge in the wood caused by the heavy frame around the painting. The serene face of the Tohunga stared up at him and for a moment he felt like throwing it onto the floor in disgust. 'Damn! Who the hell put the thing here anyway?' Ariki's face seemed to be studying the government official. 'Old man, you've been the cause of trouble, one way or the other.' Then he laughed at himself and replaced the heavy painting carefully onto the desk. At the same time a sharp stab of pain shot up his leg. Looking down he noted a red stain on the hand-knotted carpet depicting the English countryside, the offending blood coming from a deep cut in his foot. Adding to his repertoire of vitriol he hobbled over to his chair and pulled a cord which rang a bell inside the staff quarters. Mrs. Stanford, the housekeeper, entered the room.

'Sorry to wake you up like this, Margaret.' He pointed to his foot, then to the painting on his desk. 'It fell off the wall, must have broken something.'

'Don't worry Sir, just take a deep breath and I'll have a look, give me a minute.'

The housekeeper re-entered with some bandages, iodine and potassium permanganate. 'The cut's quite deep, but you'll live–just.'

'That's a relief. We'll take the …'

'Never mind that for the moment, just take a deep breath and hold on.' She daubed the wound with a large wad of cotton wool and then blew vigorously onto the wound while the agent, following his ministering angel's advice, gripped the arms of his chair in absolute agony as the raw iodine sterilized the cut.

Once his foot was heavily bandaged and elevated onto the desk, the housekeeper walked charily round the desk. 'Well, here's the reason why you cut your foot, Sir.' She held up a large shard of pink, crystal glass off the carpet. 'The present from the Austrian ambassador last year, and one of the governor's prized possessions. If you stay like that sir, I'll get a couple of the security men to help you back up the stairs.'

'No need for that Margaret, I'll sleep over there.' He pointed to the large sofa at one end of the room.

'That will be fine, better than struggling up the stairs.'

'Thank you Margaret, sorry to get you up at this time.'

'That's what I'm here for Sir.' The resonant clock announced that it was three o'clock.

The recipient of Mrs. Stanford's efforts manoeuvred his foot carefully in the middle of two pillows and tried to relax in the dark. The throbbing in his foot would ease in half an hour or so. The lady had given him some laudanum to ease the pain.

Lying on his back, the official felt suddenly uncomfortable that the picture of Ariki was still on his desk. He would order it to be placed in the reception hall from tomorrow. Anyway it was more fitting to have it there. It would be seen by his visitors. He realised that would, in time, include Maori dignitaries from far and near. He wondered how they would take to that, the poor man being tapu and all.

How the hell did the painting fall down? It had been fixed expertly onto the wall with two solid brass fasteners. Paintings don't just jump off walls.

His housekeeper, meticulous as always, had placed the painting on the desk supported against the wall. The Tohunga's face appeared to be studying him as light slanted across the man's features half in shadow. The agent felt the urge to get up and turn the painting round, but his foot hurt too much and he felt trapped.

… apparently he can disturb the forces of nature…

He closed his eyes waiting for the first rays of light to enter the study.

TWENTY

ENGLAND

Helen Hunt looked out of the window of her country cottage in the Cotswold hills, irked to see the young reporter across the road. The routine was the same. By ten o'clock the woman would knock on her door and Helen would tell her she had nothing more to say about the Tarawera eruption. A young journalist who represented the local newspaper was hoping to make her name by getting the 'full story.' The full story was something that haunted her nights, something that was between herself and the others who were there, and not for the telling. She hardly wanted to recount it to herself.

Tarawera erupted six months ago and she had become sick to death of the procession of men and women, scribbling away with pencils on their little notepads. One woman had persisted in her attempts to get Helen to cry. Ridiculous questions like, 'My dear, how *did* you feel, it would have been *sooo* shocking....' Helen had laughed cynically in her face and slammed the door shut.

She had stopped reading their reports about that night of horror, the war canoe on the lake with its grisly occupants and the wonderful person who had saved sixty people. It irritated her how the accounts in the newspapers always concentrated on the horrors and very little about the wonder of the terraces. It was as though she had lost something important in her life to think they would not be there, not anymore. Gone forever, which could not be said for her gratitude and her friendship to Sophia.

It was as though the shock of that night, the heavy hand of fear, had increased in proportion to the distance away from the event and now she knew absolutely, that the old priest's curse had followed her and would persist into her grave. At night she would start awake out of her dark dream, haunted by those men they had seen in the ancient sea-craft, entities of great height and stature with cadaverous faces, dark abominable inhabitants of a long-lost tribe, somewhere out in that land that the indigenes had named in their language, 'Aotearoa.' Translated from their language it meant, 'the land of the long white cloud.'

This morning she went out, slipped out rather, walking across the fields behind her home and then down a small country lane into town and back the same way. She arrived back, relieved to see that the young woman, the reporter from the 'Morning Mail,' had left for the day. Thank heaven for that! Now she could actually go into her house via the front door for a change.

The white envelope lay on the carpet, almost as if it was alive and would jump up and reveal its contents. She picked it up off the carpet. The envelope was slightly heavier than the normal letter-post and she jumped at the involuntary sound of her own voice. 'My goodness, a New Zealand postmark. What's this then?' A rare event as the only letters for her these days were the annual postcards at Christmas from her brother in Wales and one or two from her friends in the bridge club. She hadn't been to bridge since she came back; she really would have to pull herself together and get out of the doldrums.

She had to admit that she was a little excited at the prospect of a letter from New Zealand. What a thing! Who on earth would have written from there? She brewed a strong pot of tea and settled herself in a cane chair in the sunlight of her back garden, staring at the white envelope. You could see it had come from a long way, there was some bruising on the envelope and the corners had been bent and smudged. Helen Hunt picked up a knife and slid it under the flap. Turning the page over she began to read.

My dear Helen,

This is from your friend, Te-Paea Hinerangi, better known as Sophia.

I remembered you from the good days when we actually had something to guide people to. I hope that you are well and have got over the shock by now. If you haven't, don't worry dear you won't be the only one. I've slipped something into the letter which I am about to post from Rotorua, that was the small town you stopped at, before coming to Te Wairoa.

People have started to call it the 'buried village.' None of my tribe go there now, they regard the area as tapu. In our language that means forbidden. The English use a similar word, taboo. Same thing. Really, you have to laugh at fortune. I live in Rotorua now and, would you believe, they installed me here as the chief guide, same job but a different venue.

You were one of our small group on the lake that day who, how can I put it, saw what we saw. An event, I think you'll agree with me, experienced by very, very few on this earth. If you have some rather unsettling moments about that experience, please don't worry, we all do, it's only human nature. We'll get over it, have no fears on that account, Helen. These things can stay in the mind for a while but they will go and frankly, leave us stronger than we were before. Anyway, to make sure you will be safe I've enclosed something in the envelope, we call it a Hei-tiki. Keep it in your home, it will protect your house and bring you peace and happiness. It's actually made of greenstone jade but shaved thin by Maori carvers, so you can wear it as a pendant.

Well, that's all from me.

Best wishes for the future.

Your friend

Sophia.

Helen Hunt removed the gift from the envelope. Sophia had attached a bright red cord to the pendant. The face of the Tiki had large eyes and the stone felt smooth to the touch. Real greenstone, what a lovely thing! Without thinking she placed it round her neck. She looked in the mirror and against her skin the greenstone artefact looked good. *'It will protect you. ...These things leave us stronger than we were before.'*

Helen turned away and got out the few items she had bought from the shop, humming to herself. That night the ghouls that tormented her dreams came in briefly, even then they were fragmented, losing their abominable power over her and she saw them only in brief snatches. By the third night she slept, dreamless and uninterrupted by the undead that had fled for all time, leaving her in peace.

The fact was they hadn't altogether vanished from her conscious mind but that she–*understood.* Like an epiphany, a revelation of what it was to be drawn into a separate place, a dimension or a universe outside of herself, and it gave her a reality, perhaps a strength too that had been outside the scope of her thinking. Now she realised that she and the others had been privileged to be a part of this unique event.

The young reporter at her gate left the next day. Helen told her there was no more to tell and that she was wasting her time. There were plenty of stories in the world for a young reporter to find but not at *her* front door.

She re-joined the bridge club, finding she had more zest than at any other time.

TWENTY-ONE

RANGATIRA KEEPA-TE-RANGI-PUAWHE.

After six months the rescue party stopped coming to Te Wairoa and the outlying districts. Keepa, along with his tribe, the Tuhourangi Maori, had moved away from the nothingness of their village and had been amicably settled in Rotorua. The place was called 'Whakarewarewa,' and there was an abundance of hot pools, boiling mud and one large geyser. His people had initiated the tourist business, but it would take them a number of years to settle. Not all of his tribe would go there and so he spent time going to nearby Ngapuna. The rest had decided to leave for Thames, a territory much further away.

None of this was anything like the great Te Tarata and certainly nothing like Otukapuarangi or indeed the lakes before the eruption, and he felt deeply for his tribe, scattered far from their homeland. One or two folk had rather unkindly commented that now the Tuhorangi people would have to work for a living. Their comments, apart from being unjust, made no sense. His tribe had worked hard enough, organizing the tours and entertaining the tourists. For now they had become refugees, having to adapt to life and circumstances foreign to them. Anyway it was not all bad, they still had thermal waters to bathe in and cook their food, and places to catch fish. Tourists would come, eventually. Besides they were all tangata whenua, all tied to the land.

He stood on a small promontory midway between Lake Rotokakahi and Tikitapu, alone, with only the sound of a gentle breeze that came and went. The waters here had cleared, much of the volcanic ash had been washed back into the earth and in the soil's new fertility, grass was beginning to cover the ground and the first saplings of the great trees that covered the land had sprouted through the earth.

He stood for a long time, staring across the waters and the forests. Today the sun was warm and it reflected the blue and green from the lakes on either side of him. He heard his horse whinny from where he had tethered it, inside a small thicket of flax and ponga fern.

Sometimes he thought of that terrible night when the four white-hot cones that had generated the destruction of his tribe's homeland had exploded out of the mountain one after another. He and Mr McRae had done their utmost to help as many Maori and pakeha as they could and indeed the government had praised and subsequently honoured both men for their work that night. Apparently McRae had gone to live in Auckland, a long distance from here. One day he must go to visit him, for they had been firm friends. Tuhoto had wanted to destroy the tavern, he had mentioned this to McRae at the time and they had both laughed. Well, the old man did destroy the tavern, the village and the vast fertile tracks of land surrounding their home.

He had heard from England that his daughter was doing splendidly. A good thing he did that night, alone in the dark, exhausted, then hearing William calling out his daughter's name. He found it painful now to think of what had happened: fire sweeping through the land, hot winds, a deadly, orange hail of rock, dead people and finally the hot ash and lava obliterating everything... unstoppable, until the mountain had exerted every last atom of its destructive power in its malefic intent to plunder that which had been the most beautiful thing of this earth... destruction... fire... storm... havoc...

In the distance the call of a water bird dispelled the turmoil from his mind. A few land birds had come back here and he heard the resonant call of a kokako sounding across the new growth, in parts of the forest that had survived.

A thin wind sprang up, sending ripples across the lake. It rustled through the small bushes and from the nearby forest he heard it passing through the trees.

Keepa Rangipuawhe listened again and now he heard, or thought he heard, a whisper through the air. Was it coming through the trees? But it seemed to rise up from the lake itself. At first it sounded like the wind in its passage through the heavy branches and the dense foliage, then it was as though a voice had become disengaged from the trees, from the bush, from the lake and was speaking, to him. A whisper but clear and now he *could* hear it. The voice was indeed familiar and he recognized immediately the voice of Ariki, the Tohunga. At first he thought that he was being fanciful but no, he heard it clearly, close to him, too clear to be a trick of the imagination. And because he understood the power of the old priest he knew and believed that he spoke.

'Listen,' said the voice, 'hear the land speak. This is the beauty that I spoke of, that you and your tribe have lost, but things go and things come again. Listen! It will come back, all of it.'

The trees across the lake said it, the tui that fed on the new nectar from the kowhai and the pohutukawa sang its refrain as it tumbled and jerked in erratic flight across the sky. Bees joined in the chorus and a monarch butterfly fluttered its wings across the lake, stitching, stitching together the manifest voices that were the dreams of humanity, the dreams of his people, and the refrain was taken up across the land as the lakes and the entire forest beyond breathed out, and its incense of hope, of abundance yet to come, rose towards the sky.

'Hear it and believe, Rangatira.'

He stood for a long time in the absolute silence, seeing the beauty of the great lakes, blue on this side, green on that.

Keepa Te Rangi-puawhe turned, wrapping his cloak around his shoulders and made for home.

Te-Mutu.

Glossary of Maori names.

Aotearoa. Original name for New Zealand.

Hara. A serious offence involving the breaking of a tapu.

Kanga. A Curse.

Matae Atua. The result of a fatal curse pronounced by a Tohunga.

Makutu. Sole power of a Tohunga, to place a fatal curse.

Otukapuarangi. Pink Terrace.

Rangatira. Supreme head of a tribe.

Rotokakahi-Tikitapu. The blue and green lakes.

Te Tarata. The white terrace.

Tamahoi. The mythical giant residing in Tarawera Mountain

Tautangata. Servants of the pakeha - a reversal of roles.

Tangata whenua. People of the land. Indigenous peoples.

Tohunga. A Maori priest.

Waka Tuau. War Canoe.

Utu. Retribution

Whare. Maori dwelling.

Quantum field. 'Anyone who is not shocked by quantum theory does not understand it.' Niels Bohr.

'The mind not only penetrates the quantum field but actively participates in it. Thus human consciousness may have the potential to awaken quanta and turn them into substance.'

The Dogs of Kali

Muhammad, a warrior king from the 13th century has stolen a time key and is hell bent on world domination. His tampering with time has awakened Kali, the goddess of death, attended by her dogs of destruction. Can John, assisted by the beautiful Sati, re-discover his former power as the time lord from the 13th century and stop Muhammad?

Available on Amazon Kindle

Daughters of Rajasthan

Blood spills in the desert sands of India as a powerful man fights to steal the throne from the rightful prince. But Fate steps in with two women who are equally powerful in their own way.

Available on Amazon Kindle

Land of the First Sun
A saga of spies, terrorists, air and ground battles in Afghanistan, submarines in the pacific. The timely discovery of a secret agent by Detective Chief Inspector Pascoe, leads to the destruction of the Taliban army in their efforts to rule Afghanistan and the subsequent death of the terrorist mastermind.

Other novels are in production

If you enjoyed this story please consider posting a brief review on Amazon to help other readers to find the book.

Thank you!